A VOW OF LUST AND FURY

TAINTED VOWS BOOK ONE

LP LOVELL

A Vow of Lust and Fury
Copyright ©2021 by LP Lovell

Cover Model: Sol
Photographer: Wander Aguiar
Cover Design: Yoly Cortex
Editor: Stephie Walls

❀ Created with Vellum

"She was an angel seeking chaos. He was a demon seeking peace." – Author unknown.

1

GIO

W ith an ominous creak of hinges, I opened the basement door and stepped into a torture scene. Literally.

A single light bulb hummed overhead, casting shadows over the bleak cinder block walls and the unconscious man bound to a chair in the center of the room. Once-white bandages that covered a relatively minor gunshot wound in his gut were now red, and as the metallic scent of blood infiltrated my senses, I became high on the violence of it all.

My enforcer, Jackson, paced before him in the small space, a demented smile on his face and his bare chest smeared crimson. Judging by the array of neat slices and copious amounts of blood covering our prisoner, Jackson had thoroughly indulged in the task of extracting the information I wanted.

The guy was found beside the bodies of two of our men and an empty truck that should have been filled with cocaine. Our cocaine. Usually, I'd be far removed from such issues, but that was the third shipment this month. Whoever was brave enough to take from us was brazen. And fucking stupid. No one had dared challenge us in years, and for good reason. Retribution would be swift and brutal. But it was more complicated than I'd like because it had happened in Chicago. I didn't like to shit on my own doorstep by bringing drugs directly into New York. I had a tight grip on the Windy City; however, my lack of absolute control had my skin itching.

On a sigh, I pushed away from the door. "Did he tell you anything?"

"No," Jackson spat, still pacing like an agitated cat.

I wasn't surprised. If I were going to steal a shipment from us, I'd hire someone who couldn't be associated with it, someone who knew very little, because the consequences for such a slight would be grave.

My phone vibrated in my pocket, and I glanced at a message from one of my underbosses, Tommy. One word: Irish. Followed by a screenshot of a list of bank transactions to one Mr. Steven White. Also known as the sack of leaking blood in front of me. The money came from an account under McGinty holdings. A "legitimate" business of the Irish Mob in Chicago.

We hadn't had any issues with them recently, although we did have Patrick O'Hara's cousin, Finnegan, killed a few years back. Irish and Italian relations were always tentative. Now I had to work out if it was an act of opportunity or war. As much as I wanted heads to roll for the sheer fucking audacity, war was bad for business, and if there was one thing I didn't do, it was act rashly. There was one way to find out...

"Kill him."

Within seconds, the captive's throat was nothing more than a slash of red, blood pouring down his broken body. A kindness, really, given Jackson's propensity for torture and his dark mood consuming every inch of air in the room.

"Send his head to Patrick O'Hara's bar," I ordered before leaving the room and ascending the stairs into the main house.

Paddy O'Hara knew better, or at least he should have. How he reacted would tell me what I needed to know. I made my way into the office and closed the door, inhaling the scent of old books and leather as I poured myself a bourbon. The smoky flavor burned down my throat, taking the edge off my temper. The last thing I needed right now was issues in Chicago. I was down several shipments, and product shortages had repercussions—loss of business, competitors moving in, violence, discord, power plays...

I fell behind my desk and downed the drink. The entire situation felt off, but I couldn't put my finger on it. War was coming. I could feel it, taste the coppery tang of blood on the wind, and part of me relished in it. I smiled at the thought of Paddy O'Hara opening a box to find a severed head inside. I did it to send a message, but more than that, I did it because I could.

———

My gaze drifted over the city lights far below, so far removed from up here in my penthouse. Classical music drifted through the surround sound, and I drew in a cleansing breath, trying to find a moment of clarity in the newfound chaos.

The Irish sent us back the soldier who had delivered the head. In pieces. Then they took another shipment worth in excess of a quarter of a million. A shipment to a private airfield that no one should have known about. So that meant, not only were the Irish fucking me in the ass, but I had a rat.

I could practically feel the testosterone and violence pumping around the room the second Jackson stepped inside the penthouse. He took the death of a soldier personally. We all did. It was a blood debt. More than that, though, it meant we had an enemy who did not fear us, and those were few and far between these days.

Turning to face him, I unfastened my jacket and strode to the couch. Tommy filed in behind him, the flames from the fire flickering over the grim expression on his face.

"I had an interesting phone call this evening," I started as Jackson took a seat.

"Was it the Irish groveling for their fucking lives?" he asked, a twisted smile pulling at his lips.

"Grovelling implies remorse, and our dismembered soldier would suggest a distinct lack of that, Jackson."

He growled at me like a damn dog.

"Well? Don't keep us in suspense," Tommy said, moving over to the bar to make a drink.

"It was Sergio Donato." The leader of the Chicago family contacting me...it was almost unexpected. *Almost*.

We stayed out of Outfit business, and though the Chicago family had once enjoyed a mutually beneficial relationship with the previous "management" of the old Famiglia here in New York, we had long since branded ourselves the black sheep of the Italian Mafia. However, their interest provided an opportunity. One where I kept my hands squeaky clean.

"Apparently, he's also lost product to the Irish in the last few weeks." I took a seat on the opposite couch and propped my ankle on my knee. "He proposes an alliance."

Tommy sat on the arm, swirling the amber liquor around the glass. "Why? The Outfit and the Irish Mob have fought for decades, and they'll keep fighting—"

"Unless the scale of power were weighted in one of their favor." I lifted a brow. "Donato wants coke. We have the secure shipping routes. He doesn't."

I'd already thought of all the ways we could take advantage of this and run them past Nero. He was technically the boss, but Nero was built for war, not peace. He would paint the streets of Chicago red with a smile on his face if I let him, and that was one thing I could not risk. I'd worked too hard. There was only so much the senators and district attorney I paid off could overlook before suspicion would fall on them.

"For now, we lend him manpower, guns. They do the dirty work, handle the mob while we take very little risk. In exchange, we sell them coke at a ten percent profit."

"You know we make fifty everywhere else." Tommy frowned.

I cocked a brow. "That's why we won't actually be upholding that part."

"You're going to fuck them over," Tommy groaned.

I was going to do more than fuck them over, but I kept that to myself. They just needed to focus on the next steps, not the next twenty. My long-term plans were often susceptible to change depending on how successful the short-term ones were.

A twisted smile covered Jackson's face. "I don't care, as long as I get to kill someone. Two years of sitting around... Fucking peace," he mumbled under his breath.

Tommy snorted. "Since when do you just sit around? You tortured that guy and cut off his head two days ago."

Jackson sniffed, folding his arms over his chest until his holster looked like it was about to rupture beneath his bulk. "It's not the same. No one fights back anymore."

I pinched the bridge of my nose, praying for patience. "That's kind of the point."

"So, we just form an alliance with The Outfit, and that's it? It'll all get handled." Tommy pressed before tipping back his drink.

Anger lanced through me at the thought of what that alliance would cost me, what Sergio Donato demanded. It was like lava moving through my veins, but this was not an opportunity I would pass up. If I were going to agree to his terms, I was getting a lot more out of it than I knew he was willing to give. That was the problem with trying to chain a lion while he seemed weak. A lion was never weak, and he would tear out your throat. I would bleed Donato dry when it suited me, and his precious alliance couldn't save him.

"I'm handling it."

An hour later, I was alone, and the ping of my phone was loud in the silence of my apartment. I opened the message from one of my contacts. I'd asked him to get me everything he could find on one Miss Emilia Donato, niece of Sergio Donato. The information on her was barely more than a few sentences. Nineteen years old. Pulled out of some fancy school at age sixteen, then home-schooled. Two brothers, both Made. The details of her life were scarce.

Which meant I knew absolutely nothing about my soon-to-be wife. The thought did not sit well, but this was Donato's price and one I couldn't negotiate my way out of for once. This was the old way of sealing alliances, a half-assed guarantee forged upon the notion that corrupt men would have a degree of honor and not turn on "family." But family was not a ring and false vows or even blood. Family was those willing to die beside you.

My loyalty could not be bought by Donato or anyone else. If there was one thing I was good at, though, it was the politics of it all. So, I would go through with his marriage. He'd sell his niece into the lion's den, and with her virginity, he'd assume he was buying a seat at the table. All he would buy was a place bowing at my fucking feet. And the girl? She would serve a purpose, but I wouldn't touch her. She'd be taken care of until I no longer needed her, a pretty pawn locked in a tower. And she'd accept it because she had been bred to submit, trained to serve. The thought both annoyed and excited me.

When I closed my eyes, I pictured a faceless girl spread out for me, submissive, ready to take whatever I gave her. My dick hardened, and I forced the image away, a trace of disgust rising through the layer of indifference I lived in. That girl wouldn't be much better than a whore, stripped of choice, sold to whoever her father deemed fit. And the fact that *I* was what The Outfit deemed fit, with my reputation…it didn't say a lot for how much Sergio Donato valued his niece. But that was my line—thick, black, and unpassable. Choice. I wanted willing submission, for a woman to beg for my dick, not a terrified virgin. Still, the primal part of me roared at the thought of her blood on my cock.

2

EMILIA

Water pressed in around me, the silence in the darkness absolute. Cold. Peaceful. My skin numbed, and my mind emptied as my lungs screamed for air. I had been right here so many times and wondered what would happen if I just opened my mouth and inhaled the cool waters. It was a dark whisper in the back of my mind, a curiosity I would never indulge. When my heart pattered beneath the rush of adrenaline, I kicked my legs and broke the surface. Brilliant sunshine assaulted my vision just in time for me to take in the wooden jetty and the figure now hurtling along it. My brother, Renzo, spotted me, and a wicked grin crossed his lips as he launched into the air. I screamed when he cannon-balled into the lake only a few feet away from me.

"Asshole."

He laughed as he surfaced, and I splashed him before swimming to the jetty and hauling myself out of the water. Sunlight glittered over the lake that seemed to stretch endlessly to the horizon—the jewel of Chicago, and for me, the only decent thing about my home. Not that I'd ever really been allowed to explore the city. My parents' lakeside mansion was my own personal prison.

Renzo splashed me as he lazily backstroked past in his ridiculous flamingo swim shorts. I couldn't help but laugh a little. My youngest brother was pretty much the only person who could bring a smile to my face these days.

"Is there a reason you're annoying me?"

"Yep. Dad wants to see you in his office. *Dun-dun-dun,*" he hummed dramatically.

With a roll of my eyes, I lay down on the jetty, and he laughed. Renzo had given up trying to get me to obey my father years ago. "How long do you think it will be until Luca shows up?"

My father would absolutely send my oldest and most-loyal brother to retrieve me when Renzo didn't return.

"I decided to forgo waiting for you to fail, Renzo."

I jerked upright and glanced over my shoulder at the sound of Luca's voice. Dammit, not even any time to give him the runaround.

His great hulking form was planted on the jetty, blocking my path. I'd have to swim the width of Lake Michigan to escape him. I narrowed my eyes at him, trying to—

"Emilia," he growled like a damn bear. "Don't even think about it." He tried to seem menacing, but I didn't miss the way his hands had subtly moved to cover his crotch. He might have been big, but I was fast, and he knew it. "Father wants to see you. If you fight me, you know I'll catch you in the end, and you'll just make it worse on yourself."

On a sigh, I glanced at Renzo, and he smirked as though he could read my mind. Sometimes I liked to fight on pure principle, but Luca was right; there was no getting out of it in the end. And just when I was having a nice day.

"See, I did relay the request," Renzo said, swimming up to the jetty and hoisting himself out of the water.

If I'd asked him to run off into the woods and hide from Luca and Father with me, he would have, though, and that was why Ren was my favorite. He might have been Made and indoctrinated into my family's crime cult, but he was fun and loyal.

Snatching my sundress from the ground, I pushed to my feet and approached Luca. His black suit was firmly in place as always, devoid of any personality. Just how my father wanted him. It was ninety degrees, for Christ's sake. I could literally see the sweat rolling down his temple. His near-black eyes were fixed anywhere but on my bikini-clad body as I tugged my dress over my head.

Luca fell into step beside me, towering over me as we made our way toward the house. The strip of sand at the shore crept up to perfectly manicured lawns that were a thick carpet beneath my bare feet. Sprinklers swayed and danced, catching in the sun and painting the air in rainbows like this was some kind of Disney movie. And it sure as hell wasn't that.

"You know, I have a phone. You don't have to come and personally escort me to some stupid meeting," I said as I stepped through the back door.

Luca let out a snort. "Emilia, I would never give you warning."

"So untrusting."

We passed through the hallway lined with abstract artwork and marble floors. So pretentious. So...my mother. We were only a few meters from my father's office door when Luca pulled me to a halt. I glanced up at the frown marring his face.

"Emilia, Uncle Sergio is in there."

I felt the color drain from my face along with any bravado I might have been feeling.

"Just... behave, okay? I know you hate this family, but don't get on his bad side." And with those reassuring words about my psycho, mafia boss uncle, my traitorous brother dragged me to the door, knocked, and shoved me inside.

When I entered my father's office, the scent of cigars greeted me. Father sat behind the huge desk that dwarfed everything else in the room, a haze of smoke gently swirling through the sunlight that poured through the window.

This room always brought a sense of nostalgia, memories of moments spent sitting on my father's lap in that very chair as he read from first editions of Charles Dickens and Lewis Carroll. That was before, though. My father was no longer that man, and whatever innocent adoration I'd once held for him had long since been torn away. Now, it wasn't my father who drew my attention but my uncle. He leaned against the front of the desk, arms folded as he watched me approach. His shrewd gaze swept over me, the void in his eyes making me as uncomfortable as ever before he sneered. I had no doubt that my beach wear and soaked-through dress were not considered suitable attire for this asshole's presence.

The charcoal-gray suit he wore was nearly the same color as his neatly combed hair, clinging to a wiry body. Sergio Donato could almost pass as a businessman if it weren't for the ice in his eyes, a kind of cold that dug into your soul and pried you apart from the inside. Uncle Sergio had always scared me. When I was younger, I thought he was the Scar to my father's Mufasa. Little did I know that Disney had gotten it wrong, and the bad guy always wore the crown, not that my father was some regal saint.

I could feel my uncle's gaze burning into the side of my face as I took a seat in front of the desk. My heart let out a thundering beat that felt an awful lot like the symphony of my impending demise, and I gritted my jaw, forcing my figurative armor into place.

"Emilia," my father began. His dark gaze bore into me, daring me to misbehave in front of his brother. "You are to be wed." Just like that. He said the words like he was discussing what we were having for dinner.

Of course, I had thought this might happen at some point; that I'd be standing right here in this room while my parents tried to sell me off and buy something favorable with my virginity. The fact that Father would even try to do this to me after everything… But no, the same man who had read *Alice in Wonderland* to me now offered nothing but indifference in the face of my worst nightmare. Maybe this was what it took to stand at the top of The Outfit. No heart. No soul.

Anger punched through the horror, licking up my spine until it took everything in me to keep my expression smooth. Emotions weren't welcome here, and the only thing that would garner me respect right now was strength. I'd long ago been robbed of the innocent belief that women in the mafia were valued. That men like Uncle Sergio and my father could and would protect us. It was bullshit. Women in the mafia were assets, protected for their worth. Nothing else.

I stared straight at my father, squaring my shoulders. "No."

Uncle Sergio shifted to his full height and turned his back on me as he moved to the window, as though I were unworthy of his full attention. "Your father believes you are capable of doing your duty for The Outfit, *Emilia*." He spat my name like it offended him. "This marriage is an important one and would be most beneficial with a Donato bride." Of which there was only one left—thanks to him and my father. "Of course, Matteo Romano still believes he is also owed a Donato bride."

Just the sound of that man's name was like a shot of ice into my veins, paralyzing my ailing heart.

Sergio glanced over his shoulder. "Seeing as the first one was…defunct."

"My sister was not defunct!" I snapped while my father said nothing. Not a word.

My uncle's lips twitched, mocking me, enjoying my suffering. "Would you rather marry him?"

My temper bubbled beneath my skin, wild and volatile, and I vowed to myself right then that one day…one day, I would kill that man. He would die in the flames of fury he had stoked in me for years.

"Even you cannot make me speak vows to that piece of shit, old man."

My uncle moved like a snake, the back of his hand colliding with my cheek. Blood exploded in my mouth as he gripped my throat, yanking me to my feet until my body was flush against his. Again, my father said not a damn word. And me, I smiled in my uncle's face because I'd made him lose control and gotten a reaction.

"If you will not speak those vows, then you will be his whore. To fuck and break. I'm sure he won't mind either way, and you're no use to me if you won't marry."

My smile faded, and hot, angry tears stung the backs of my eyes as blood trickled from my split lip. I tried to be brave, not to back down to these men and their threats, but this was one I couldn't hide my fear of—Matteo Romano.

My uncle knew he'd won, and a smug smile pulled at the corners of his lips as he shoved me back into the chair. I sucked in a ragged breath as he smoothed a hand down the front of his suit.

"Good. Now…your marriage."

I had no comeback, no words, no fight. He'd played his trump card, and in this moment, he had me. Because really, how was I supposed to stand up to a man like him? Right now, I couldn't, but I could bide my time. I might not have succeeded in escaping my family, but if they wanted me to marry—

"You will marry Giovanni Guerra. He is consigliore and underboss to Nero Verdi."

My heart dropped.

I hated everything that encompassed our world—the traditions, the codes, the false decency. Those were the thick, black lines of my life, placing me in a tiny box. But Nero Verdi and Giovanni Guerra…the New York Famiglia had no lines. I'd heard the rumors. They killed women and children, obliterated their competition so ruthlessly, few would or could stand against them. Least of all, my uncle and father. Why the hell was he trying to ally with the Famiglia? But of course, the answer was obvious. Power. Power he was willing to buy with me. The thought made me sick. On more than one occasion, my father had said that the Famiglia had no honor, no code. Although, honestly, I'd seen what "honorable" men did, and that word didn't mean a thing to me anymore. Still, Father was willing to sell me to men he himself branded as monsters, and I couldn't deny that it hurt.

Uncle Sergio watched my silent monologue with narrowed eyes. "I see you know the name."

"Yes," I said, forcing my voice to remain steady.

He grabbed my chin, thumb swiping over my bloody lip and making me wince before he forced my gaze to his. He towered over me, and I wanted to stand, but I also didn't want him to think he intimidated me. "Matteo wants an unruly whore to break. Giovanni Guerra will expect a proper Outfit wife. Obedient, submissive, one who knows her place. Which are you, Emilia? A wild whore or a mafia princess?"

Neither. I was just a girl who wanted to be free of this life. But this…Matteo…this was a punishment, leverage to make me marry Giovanni Guerra, and it was truly cruel in a way only my uncle could be.

"Do you hate me so much, Uncle?"

He released my chin. "Don't be childish. We all have our duty, girl." He grasped my hand and tugged me to my feet before kissing both my cheeks like he hadn't just hit me and threatened to let that animal rape me. "You'd do well to remember it."

Oh, I'd remember this well. I'd carve it on my heart and wear the scar until the day I could repay Uncle Sergio the favor. He flashed me a knowing grin before turning to my father.

They shook hands, and the second the door clicked shut behind him, I picked up a paperweight off the desk and launched it after him, leaving a dent in the door.

"Fuck!" Angry tears stung the backs of my eyes. I wanted to kill him. And my father. And Matteo. And this Giovanni. Men who thought they could sell me or buy me.

My father turned his back on me and stared out the window, ignoring my outburst. A curse slipped under his breath before he faced me. The coldness had left his eyes, replaced with obvious stress. "You cannot talk to him like that, Emilia. Your uncle will not be as lenient on you as I am."

"*Lenient?* You just sold me like a damn horse in your stable. And if I don't marry this guy, I'm sure you'll stand by and hand me over to be raped by that creature."

"Enough!" he roared, slamming both hands onto the desk.

He didn't scare me, though. I'd known for years that my father was a small man. I'd long since lost all respect for him.

"Why? Does it bother you, hearing the truth? That you already let it happen to Chiara." I moved closer until my thighs bumped the desk. "That you failed to protect the one person you should have at all costs. Am I as disposable as she was because I have a vagina?" My voice cracked, giving away my hurt through my attempt at holding a front.

He grabbed the edge of the desk, dropping his head forward as though the weight of the world rested on him. "The Famiglia are…uncouth, but Giovanni is honorable enough."

I snorted. "Tell me, Father, would you consider yourself honorable?"

He glanced at me, his lips pressing in a thin line.

"Yeah, your version of honor doesn't mean a thing to me."

His jaw clenched, the muscle ticcing, but he said nothing. I wanted to cut him, emotionally and physically. I wanted him to hurt like I did because some deep-seated part of me was still pathetically wishing my father would protect me from a world I'd never asked to be a part of. But if wishes were horses, beggars would ride.

"I love you, Emilia. This is for the best."

There were a thousand things I wanted to say, but it had all been said before, all fallen on deaf ears. Because his loyalty was to his brother, not his daughter.

I turned and walked toward the door. "We both know that's a lie. I'm nothing more than a whore to you and your boss." I heard his sharp intake of breath as I yanked open the door.

I had barely made it into the hall before my father's footsteps pounded after me, and he snatched my wrist in a bruising grip. He didn't even say anything, just dragged me to the door halfway down the corridor, taking a key from his pocket to unlock it. My pulse ticked up, panic threading through my veins, but I refused to let any of my fear show on the outside. He opened it and dragged me down the stairs before unlocking the door at the bottom and shoving me inside the small, windowless room. There was only a bed, a toilet, and a shelf full of books. Nothing else. There was a time when I would be crying now, begging and pleading with him not to leave me here. Those pleas always fell on deaf ears, though, so I learned not to show weakness to men who had no mercy.

I turned to face him in the doorway, and he closed the distance between us, stroking a hand over my hair.

"Emilia," he said softly.

For a moment, I held the vain hope that he might say something to show he actually gave a shit. It was the sad need of a daughter who still held a glimmer of hope that her father actually loved her.

"You will marry Giovanni Guerra."

I stepped back, and his hand fell away.

"Matteo wants you, and if you do not learn your place, then I fear Sergio will agree to Romano's terms. He will not risk bartering an unruly bride for a fragile alliance. Please. I do not want to lose another daughter."

"You already have," I said as I took another step back and another until I fell onto the bed that was as familiar to me as the luxury one upstairs. That tentative hope shattered inside my chest as I remembered I was truly alone.

My father let out a long breath. "You will stay in here until you come to your senses." Then he shut the door, the click of the lock enough to stoke the flames of my fear. The four walls pressed in on me, and there was no escape.

No one was going to save me from this because, in this story, there was no white knight or prince charming, only a sea of villains, and I, cast amongst them.

3

EMILIA

ONE WEEK LATER...

My heart was pounding a staccato beat as the bright lights of Chicago faded in the side mirror. With Renzo's help, I'd fled my own engagement party, ran while everyone was distracted and the guards were letting guests on and off the property. Nothing but open road lay before us, and a weight lifted off my chest, allowing me to breathe properly for what felt like the first time since I'd first understood what my father did. It was the untainted air of freedom.

I'd run before and not even made it out of the city, but this time was different. Right now, this rusted old sedan felt like the sweetest freedom, and even the stench of cigarettes and fast food in here couldn't shadow my elation. But one thing could, and that was my brother sitting behind the wheel, running with me. I knew he was the only reason I'd even made it this far, but when I accepted his offer to help me at the house, I'd never expected him to stay with me. The guilt was like a knife twisting between my ribs.

"Ren…"

He turned down the radio, the twang of country music fading into a low hum. "Don't start again, Emi."

"You could just drop me at a bus station and go back. Dad will forgive you."

The glow from the lights on the dashboard played over the angry set of his jaw. "No. I'm coming with you. End of—"

"You know they're coming for us, Renzo."

The moment Giovanni Guerra turned up at that party and his fiancée was nowhere to be found, they'd hunt us like a pack of dogs on a game trail.

"He's going to come for me. I should have met him, feigned a headache or something. Bought us more time."

He shook his head. "No. You're right, he *is* going to come for you. I will do everything possible to keep you from him but trust me, it's better for him to think you ran blindly from marriage than you don't want to marry *him*. It will be less of a stain on his honor."

There it was again, talk of honor from heinous men. That was even more reason for Renzo to go home, though.

"I can do this alone, Ren—"

"You really think I'm going to leave you to fend for yourself?"

"Leave me with a gun."

He snorted, though there was no humor in the sound. "If it gets to that point, you're already fucked. You need me to help you, so you never have to come face to face with him."

"And if he finds us?"

He tried to hide it, but I saw the fear painted in the lines of my brother's face. He didn't answer me, though, just turned up the music and focused on the road ahead.

We had enough clothes for a week, our passports, and cash. And so, we drove through the night. At every gas station, I was looking over my shoulder, just waiting for one of my uncle's men or Giovanni to jump out like the boogeyman. We swapped cars and trudged on along the interstate until the oncoming blur of headlights reduced to intermittent big rigs. Finally, the adrenaline waned, and I drifted into a fitful sleep.

When Renzo shook me awake, the sun was rising, the last whispered pink hues of dawn fading against bright skies. In front of us was the Canadian border, like a bright, glowing safe haven. Of course, it wasn't. They'd follow us anywhere, but it at least felt safer than Chicago. Renzo thought Canada was the last place they'd expect us to go, though. Instead of crossing at the nearest point in Detroit, we'd skirted Minneapolis and crossed at Fort Frances. He flashed our passports to the border patrol, and they let us pass without issue.

The first town we came to, Renzo pulled into a Walmart parking lot, and we ditched the car, changing it out for a minivan he stole. My brother looked ridiculous behind the wheel, but for once, I was too tired and stressed to even mock him for it.

By that evening, having not slept for nearly two days, Renzo could barely keep his eyes open. My father had never let me learn to drive, or I would have gladly taken over. I guess he didn't want to give me any greater chances of running away.

After pleading with him to stop, Renzo finally pulled over at a service station, parking in a far corner at the back of the lot.

He handed me his gun. "Anyone comes, you point and shoot."

I lifted a brow. "Anyone?"

A small smile cut across his lips. "I mean, if a hot hooker rocks up—"

"You're gross."

Renzo snorted and closed his eyes. As he drifted to sleep, I noticed the stress lines that clung to his normally youthful features, even in rest. That now-familiar guilt spread over my skin like a rash. My gaze drifted out the window at an eighteen-wheeler that had pulled into the service station, its gut-heavy driver refueling himself and his vehicle. I could just get out of the car now, hitch a ride with him somewhere. Renzo could go home. Would Father punish him? Undoubtedly. But I knew he wouldn't kill him. Renzo was too important to The Outfit, an enforcer, the boss's nephew.

I reached for the door handle, and the second it clicked open, the interior light came on, startling Renzo awake. He looked around before his eyes landed on me.

"What are you doing?" he snapped, leaning over me and tugging the door shut before engaging the locks.

"I...I just needed to pee," I lied, unwilling to admit to anything that would make me seem ungrateful.

Renzo huffed out a breath. "Fine." He took the gun from me. "Come on."

And so, I earned myself the indignation of my brother waiting right outside the stall while I peed, and he lost some precious sleep to my stupidity.

That was how the next couple of days went as we steadily made our way north and farther from civilization. Cities gave way to snowy forests and lakes that looked like a mirrored doorway to some forgotten world. Despite the danger of our situation, there was a certain peace here. The vastness of it all made me feel small, a needle that could easily get lost in a haystack, and that made me feel safer. After three days on the road, Renzo finally thought it was safe enough for us to stay in a motel room for the night, and I was grateful. My back and hips were aching from being in the car.

It was late when we pulled up outside a run-down-looking motel in a tiny town. A blinking, red neon sign lingered over the gravel parking lot of a wooden building. It was quaint and kind of creepy, like something out of a Stephen King novel.

After Renzo got the key and our bags, he led me to one of the doors on the ground floor. The night air was freezing, and the jeans and heavy sweater I wore did little to keep out the chill as we crossed the lot to the room. The faded red paint was peeling from the door, and the number 6 hung at a jaunty angle. We stepped into musty, yellow walls, floral bedspreads, and worn carpet. The entire room smelled like feet, cigarette smoke, and desperation because only the most desperate souls would find themselves here, surely. I had to wonder what that made us because compared to the last two nights, this was an upgrade. I perched on the edge of the bed while Renzo set about checking the bathroom, then pulling the curtains and locking the door. I turned on the little box

TV, and the room flooded with the low hum of enthusiastic infomercials.

Renzo never let down his guard, though, standing at the window and watching the parking lot. Red light from the neon sign outside sliced through the parted curtains, highlighting the heavy circles beneath his eyes.

"You should sleep for a few hours. We need to move again," Renzo said without looking at me.

"You need to sleep, Ren, not me."

He stayed where he was, gun clutched in his hand like he was waiting for a SWAT team to storm the place. In reality, it was probably worse.

On a sigh, I got up and took a shower, the first I'd had in three days. Then I changed into my jeans and a fresh shirt because if there was one thing I knew, it was to always be prepared to have to wake from a dead sleep and run. I lay down on top of the floral bedspread, unwilling to get any closer to the mattress that probably had more bodily fluids on it than a community bathroom. My gaze trailed over the silhouette of my brother's back, wishing I could take some of the strain that pulled his muscles tight. Not that I could blame him.

I could practically feel the wolves nipping at our heels, their hot breath lingering over my skin. An image of my uncle's face was constantly at the forefront of my mind, the rage painted in his cold eyes along with the glee he would find in punishing me. It was imprinted as a warning of what would happen should we get caught. And I knew exactly what my punishment would be…

"Renzo?"

"Yeah," he replied without looking at me.

"He's going to give me to Matteo, isn't he?" I whispered into the darkness.

The second I'd told him what Uncle Sergio had threatened, Renzo had vowed to get me out, even if it killed him. I hadn't taken that literally, but now I wondered if this would cost me dearly. I hadn't allowed myself to think about getting caught, but now I was thinking about the consequences. If Giovanni got us, he might kill us both. If Uncle Sergio did, then Renzo would be punished and I'd be thrown to Matteo like a chew toy to a pitbull.

"They won't catch us," Renzo said resolutely.

"But if they do…."

"Romano won't touch you, Emi. I promise." His voice broke, and my chest squeezed tight.

My worry was that Renzo would die keeping that promise and that I couldn't bear.

I woke to a weird scratching sound. Quiet. So quiet. The TV was now off, and I glanced around the dark room, trying to orientate myself. A tiny sliver of the neon-red light from outside cut over Renzo's sleeping form. That scratching sound started again, breaking through the silence that had settled over me like a blanket of needles. It was coming from the door. I sat up and reached for Renzo just as the lock clicked and the door knob turned.

"Renzo!"

Red light spilled into the room like a doorway to hell itself had opened. A single gunshot rang out, the bang deafening me as a flash lit up the darkness. Everything stopped, the scene playing out in soundless slow motion as shadowy figures suddenly filled the small room. It took a second shot for my frozen body to finally respond and roll off the bed.

My knees collided with the floor, though the pain barely registered past the adrenaline flooding my body. Through the ringing in my ears, I heard shouts and a struggle. And then everything fell ominously quiet. Renzo. I tried to force myself to move, but I was paralyzed. Years around dangerous men, yet I'd never found myself in the middle of flying bullets. Funny, how I thought I would react and the stone-cold reality of survival instinct could not be further apart. Ragged breaths slipped past my lips, my heart thrumming against my ribs like it would tear free of my chest if it could. Too loud. I was too loud, a wounded animal screaming in the midst of hunters.

Muted footsteps whispered over the threadbare carpet, and all I could do was stare at the pair of shiny dress shoes that rounded the bed and stopped in front of me. My gaze slowly raked up over the dark form of a man in a suit. Red light played over a scarred face I recognized as one of my father's capos—Stefano. He'd guarded our house before, come to birthday parties and my grandma's funeral. He'd watched me grow up… and yet his eyes were detached, merciless. I knew then he was going to kill me.

Panic clawed its way up my throat, and though I had no way to escape, desperation kicked in. I lurched to my feet and tried to scramble over the bed. He grabbed at me, and I fought, scratching and lashing out. My fist rammed into his throat like Luca had once shown me, then I jabbed my thumb into his eye. He roared and struck me in the side of the head before I was yanked by my hair. Pain radiated through my temple, and the room spun as I was dragged against his much bigger body. Hot, cigarette-tinted breath washed over my face before he spoke in my ear.

"Matteo Romano said if he can't have you, no one can."

No, no, no. The terror that had already been choking me reached a frenzied crescendo at the sound of that man's name, but really, what did it matter whether it was Matteo or my uncle? Either way, I was about to die, and honestly, there was a certain peace in that knowledge. Maybe there was something beyond this life and Chiara would be waiting for me.

That thought made it a little easier when Stefano forced me back to my knees in front of him. I stared at him in the darkness and realized that this moment felt inevitable. My family was determined to bend me until I broke, but I refused to break. I would rather be on my knees, right here, right now, than be on them for the rest of my life for a man like Matteo Romano.

With icy purpose, Stefano lifted his gun. My heart let out a furious beat as though rushing to get in its last few precious moments before it would beat no more. I closed my eyes, a trembling breath slipping from my lips as the cool barrel nudged against my forehead. A single tear tracked down my cheek, a staggered breath filled frozen lungs, and then... *bang*! My entire body jerked, and I choked on a breath, but there was no pain, no final moment, no bright light. When I opened my eyes, an angel of death stood before me, bathed in shadows, with Stefano's body at his feet and a gun in his hand. I felt like a lowly mortal bowing in front of the terrifying stranger.

Sapphire eyes met mine, not a trace of warmth to be found in them as they swept over me with the assessment of a predator weighing its next meal. He would probably kill me next, but God, he was beautiful. The most beautiful man I'd ever seen, with cheekbones that could cut glass and dark hair falling over his forehead in messy waves. Maybe I was already dead and he truly was an angel come to collect my soul. He sure as hell looked like one. The throbbing in my head intensified, and those full lips of his pressed into a tight line as I swayed side to the side slightly.

"Get the fuck away from her, Guerra," my brother spat.

Whatever weird bubble I'd been in burst and everything around me filtered in once more. I glanced across the room to where Renzo stood in front of the window, a gun pointed at… Guerra? *Giovanni* Guerra? My brother's free hand was pressed to his stomach, where blood pooled through his fingers. Another man seemed to materialize from the shadows by the door and had a weapon rammed to my brother's temple in an instant.

"Don't get excited," the newcomer said.

"Please don't hurt him," I stammered, pushing to my feet and fighting to stay there as the room warped and spun around me. "Just… just kill me but leave Renzo."

"No, Emi," Renzo practically snarled.

I looked to the one who was clearly in charge. The dark angel. The man I was supposed to marry. "Please."

His head tilted to the side, those eyes giving away nothing before he waved a hand at his companion. The other man took away Renzo's gun and dragged him outside. Deep down, I knew they'd find me and potentially kill me from the second I got into that car, so why had I bothered running? *Because you had to try*, a little voice whispered in the back of my mind.

"Come." One word, the only one he'd uttered since entering this room. It felt like a rumble of thunder in a summer storm, like static in the air promising chaos.

He took a firm hold of my arm, guiding me around the three bodies littering the motel room floor and outside into the parking lot. As adrenaline waned, I stumbled and swayed, but his grip never faltered. I was led to a waiting SUV, my brother leaning heavily against it, a red-haired guy beside him. Renzo's gaze met mine, and he gave the smallest of nods before he mouthed, "run." I wasn't going to leave him—I didn't get a chance to think on it before he threw a punch at the guy. I didn't want to leave him. Couldn't. They'd kill him.

"Run, Emi!" he shouted just as the guy hit him back.

The edge in Renzo's voice threw me into a blind panic, and I drove my knee between Giovanni's legs. I barely saw him double over before my feet were moving of their own volition. I turned and sprinted across the parking lot, tripping and stumbling as hot tears poured down my cheeks.

"Emilia!" Giovanni shouted after me.

Just fifty yards and I'd make it to the woods behind the motel. The sound of the gunshot was enough to make me stop, fear for my brother overriding everything. But then the pain registered, fire tearing through my thigh before my leg buckled. I hit the ground and glanced down at the blood rapidly soaking through my jeans. The pain was like a hot poker being rammed through my leg, and a desperate sob slipped through my lips as shoes crunched over the gravel and came to a stop beside me.

"The next time I have to chase you, it won't end well, princess." Giovanni gripped my arm and wrenched me to my feet with a cry. "Now, be a good girl before I put a bullet in your brother's head."

I whimpered and limped to the car, every step a lesson in agony. My head spun, and black spots dotted my vision as I climbed into the back seat.

Renzo was already there, gasping breaths pouring from him almost as easily as the blood that covered his stomach and soaked into his jeans. Giovanni got into the passenger seat beside the red-haired guy.

"He needs a doctor, Gio," the man said before focusing out the windshield and pulling away.

"I'll have one at the jet."

Renzo was panting, his face pale and clammy. Gently, I tugged him down until his head rested on my uninjured thigh, his distant gaze fixed on the ceiling. With a trembling hand, I stroked his sweat-damp hair and prayed to anyone who would listen not to let him die. But there was so much blood. I tugged my T-shirt over my head and wadded it up, pressing it into his stomach.

"I'm sorry," I whispered.

He had taken a bullet because of me, and if he died, I'd never forgive myself. He grasped my hand, slick fingers threading through mine, and it terrified me.

"You're fine," I said, my voice cracking under the words I didn't really believe. "You'll be okay."

Blood was spreading across the back seat. Mine and Renzo's combined, and the sight of it had a sob catching in my chest. Too much. It was too much.

He made a choked sound, and I squeezed his hand harder.

"He needs a hospital. Please!"

Giovanni glanced over his shoulder at me. "He'll be fine." That was it; then he started making calls on his phone.

I had never hated anyone as much as I hated him in that moment. But I was helpless to do anything, and that meant I might have to watch my brother die.

A low buzzing rang through my ears, and my vision swam as my head began pounding even harder. I touched my temple, and my fingers came away crimson. Damn, that hurt almost as much as the bullet in my leg. As the last dregs of adrenaline ebbed, my body became nothing but pain. When I blinked, it was in an effort to open my eyes again.

"Emilia?" Giovanni's voice sounded distant, like it was coming through a tunnel. He spat a curse as black spots danced in front of me.

And then everything went black.

4

EMILIA

I woke in the front seat of a car with someone shaking me. The first thing I noticed was it was dark, an amber light cutting through the windows and casting shadows over the concrete walls of the parking garage beyond. A foggy layer of confusion clung to me as I tried to figure out where I was and how I had gotten here. My gaze shifted to the person sitting behind the wheel of the parked vehicle. Giovanni Guerra. The sleeves of his black dress shirt were rolled up, revealing tattooed forearms, the intricate ink work seeming to swirl and shift with my hazy vision.

"Where am I?" I asked, my tongue thick in my mouth.

He didn't answer, and as the fog slowly cleared, the last few hours rushed in. The blood… The motel room…

"Renzo—"

"I would worry about yourself, princess." His voice was a low rumble of warning, a precursor of what was to come.

I had run, he had caught me, and the consequences were sure to be dire. But all I could think about was my brother. The last time I'd seen him, he was bleeding out. My own fate was as doomed as it had always been, but I never had wanted to drag Renzo with me.

Giovanni got out of the car and rounded the hood, shrugging on his suit jacket before pulling open my door. I had no idea what awaited me out there, but I knew he would drag me out if I didn't go willingly.

I swung my legs over the edge of the seat, noticing then the man's shirt that drowned me and the gaping leg of my jeans that had been cut open, my thigh bandaged. Giovanni gave me no space, his broad frame blocking my view beyond him, as though he were trying to prove that I'd never reach the big, wide world ever again. And I didn't doubt he thought that was the case. The iciness in his gaze combined with his bloody reputation made Giovanni Guerra terrifying. Only a crazy person would risk inciting that dangerous attention. I vowed then and there that I would escape him, but if he had Renzo…

"Please. Just tell me…is my brother alive?"

His silence was my only answer, and my temper spiked. He had me. He'd won. The least he could do was just tell me if I'd cost my brother his life for nothing.

My teeth clenched. "If he dies—"

"You'll what, princess?" He laughed, a cruel, cutting sound that echoed off the concrete walls of the parking garage. "The Outfit can't and won't stand against me. So, there is absolutely nothing you can or will do but submit."

The feeling of helplessness that washed over me with his words was debilitating, and I knew he was right. I was on my own. I never should have run, definitely shouldn't have let Renzo run with me. And now…now there was nothing I could do. It had changed nothing. I was still here, still my uncle's pawn. Only now, Renzo was… I cut off the thought. He couldn't be dead.

Giovanni gripped my arm and yanked me out of the car, tugging me flush against him. Pain shot up my leg as I bared weight on it, and I gritted my teeth, my gaze drifting past him and marking the exits.

"Don't do anything stupid. I'd hate to have to put another scar on your body."

"Of course." I glared at him, fruitlessly trying to pull away. "Couldn't have a scarred trophy wife." Acid dripped from my tone, and I hoped he felt my hatred. If I couldn't find a way to escape, then I might have to marry this man, but he would be under no illusion as to just how much he disgusted me.

He dragged me across the parking lot to a waiting elevator, and I was shoved inside so hard that I stumbled against the metal wall. He was right there, invading my space, the woodsy, minty smell of him washing over me. He was so close I could see the tiny flecks of gold in his sapphire irises, feel the heat of him seeping through the material of my shirt. He was beautiful. The thought was an unwanted one but no less true.

His face was perfection, his body honed, broad shoulders straining against the veil of civility that suit jacket was trying to portray. No suit could hide what he was, though—a weapon, a monster. A hand landed beside my head, caging me in just like the captive I was. Hot breath washed over my neck as he brought his lips to my ear, and I closed my eyes, trembling against the elevator wall. Fear and something foreign and unwanted slid through my veins like a drug, and I couldn't help but revel in the high of it for just a moment.

"I'll do more than just scar you, piccola." Piccola. Little one. There was something inherently disturbing about the whispered endearment mixed with a threat. "You are a means to an end. So, I suggest you behave like a good little mafia princess." He shoved away from me, and I sucked in my first full breath since I'd stepped in here.

If he thought threats would make me cower, he was sadly mistaken. I'd been threatened my whole life, and my father and uncle hadn't broken me yet. Though I could admit that Giovanni was far more terrifying.

He pressed a button on the wall panel, and the doors glided shut. I was now locked in a metal box with a man who would not hesitate to kill me. A man I was sold to and had run from. I assumed he wouldn't want a bride who had dishonored him. That he would either kill me or hand me back to my family. But he had saved me from my father's capo, so what did that mean? Were those elevator doors about to open and reveal my uncle, maybe even Matteo Romano, ready to take ownership of his new toy? Oh, God. My breaths came faster, and I thought I might throw up.

The elevator eventually stopped moving, and if he noticed me hurrying to get out of that confined space with him, he didn't say anything. We were in a hallway with marble flooring and soft music drifting through speakers. No sign of my uncle or Matteo. *Yet.* I looked around for an exit, willing to chance being shot again at this point. There was only a single door at the end of the corridor. Giovanni strode down the hallway and opened it, and for a moment, I was stunned. Beyond was an apartment that looked like it belonged in an edition of *Good Housekeeping*. The penthouse was huge, the floor-to-ceiling glass exterior offering uninterrupted views of New York. I wasn't exactly unfamiliar with wealth, but this was next level. Snapping out of my daze, I took a step back. A prison was still a prison, no matter how pretty.

His eyes narrowed like he expected me to try to run, like he wanted me to, because like any predator, he'd enjoy the chase. I could see the kitchen from here, the knife block like a glowing beacon on the counter. He was already on guard, and I'd need him to drop it a little. So, I forced myself to take a calming breath and walk inside as though I wasn't planning to ram a blade into his cold heart.

The front door closed behind me, a loud beep signaling the lock engaging. I was trapped, caught, and hopeless.

Giovanni ducked down a corridor to the right of the front door. "Come."

I waited for him to take a few steps away from me before I made a break for it, half running, half stumbling on my injured leg. It wasn't far, and yet the distance across the huge penthouse felt colossal when I knew he was at my back. My fingers hooked one of the knives before my head was snatched back by my hair. Pain ripped over my already abused scalp, and I hissed out a breath, fighting and slashing wildly as he trapped me between his body and the counter. Gripping my wrist, he squeezed until my fingers released, the blade clattering to the marble.

"That was stupid."

I panted out heavy breaths, waiting. For him to press a gun to my head, or perhaps just snap my neck.

He moved back enough to spin me around before gripping my hair once more and wrenching my head back so far that it was all I could do not to buckle under his hold. "What were you going to do, kill me?" A smirk played over his full lips as though the idea of me hurting him was amusing

"If that's what it takes to be free of you," I spat through gritted teeth, refusing to buckle or break for this man or any other. Because that was what they wanted.

"Keep trying, piccola." His eyes flashed with something feral, as though the thought excited some primal part of him. "But until you succeed, you are mine. Run again, and I will hunt you. Fight…" His grip tightened, and I winced as pain seemed to reverberate around my entire skull, a slow trickle of warm liquid running down my temple. "Now come." He released me and simply walked back to that hallway.

Wait. What?

He just called me his, threatened to hunt me…. He still intended to marry me. And that might have been scarier than the prospect of going back to Chicago. Because what kind of man kept a woman he knew was unwilling? A man who was no better than Matteo Romano. A monster.

With no other option, I followed him down that hallway, defeat a heavy weight on my shoulders. As we walked, I couldn't help but notice how tall he was, the broad expanse of his shoulders…how easily he could and had overpowered me. We passed a couple of doors before he opened one at the end of the hall and stepped inside. It was a large, windowless bedroom, and the screens casting an artificial view of the mountains were doing little to relieve the immediate sense of claustrophobia. My gaze fixed ominously on the bed, but before I could take a step back, the door clicked shut behind me. Behind us.

A whole new awareness reared its ugly head. I had been so fixated on escaping, on the possibility of my uncle or Matteo waiting for me, the thing I should have been worried about hadn't occurred to me until right then. I had run from him, but he still wanted me, and he would undoubtedly think he was owed something. Something I knew all too well that men like him were happy to take.

Giovanni slipped his jacket from his shoulders and tossed it onto a chair in the corner. That one action had all my fears bubbling to the surface until they boiled over in a manic frenzy. This was my reckoning, here, locked in a room with him. I always knew this would probably be my fate—married off and bedded by a stranger, but I was no one's whore, and I would never submit to this archaic bullshit. I took a shaky step away from him, moving across the room, though I really had nowhere to go.

A frown marred his face as he followed. "What did I say about running, princess?"

Adrenaline shot through my veins, and desperation had me scrambling to the bedside table. I picked up the lamp and yanked the cord free before throwing it at him. He batted it away easily, leaving it to smash against the floor.

"You are testing my patience." He closed the distance between us, backing me into a corner between the wall and the nightstand.

At the last second, blind panic had me diving over the bed, trying to get to the door, but he grabbed my hips and pinned me to the mattress. It felt too familiar to what Stefano had done in that motel room right before he had put a gun to my head. As though I were nothing. A possession. An unruly horse in a stable to be put down. And now Giovanni wished to take from me, to strip me of choice and will. I raged against it, all of it. I managed to roll beneath his weight before my palm met his cheek. Nails raked down his throat, and my legs flailed in the meek attempt to bring a knee up between his thighs. I was wild, determined, driven by rage and pure survival instinct.

"Enough!" He grabbed my wrists and imprisoned them above my head as his other hand clamped around my throat.

I couldn't move an inch, and tears of frustration welled as my chest heaved against his. It was pathetic how easily he'd subdued me, and it felt like a representation of my entire life. Weak. Powerless. Helpless.

"Don't make me hurt you," he whispered.

So, he wanted me to just lay there and take it? Revulsion rose in the form of bile up the back of my throat.

Just when I expected him to start tearing at my clothing, he shoved away from me. I scrambled to my feet and felt like I was standing in front of a wild animal, trying not to move, lest he take chase. Giovanni watched me for a beat longer as though trying to permanently brand his angry glare into my mind. Then he crossed the room, disappearing through a darkened doorway. The light inside blinked on, revealing a bathroom.

My panic receded bit by bit, and I felt the trickle of blood now running down my face more freely. When I reached up and touched it, I found a dressing that had soaked through. When had I cut my head? And when had someone treated it?

Giovanni placed a small box and a bowl of water on the nightstand. His cheek was red, scratches covering his neck in angry lines now dotted with blood. I'd hurt him, but he'd made no move to hurt me back…yet. Still, my uncle would have left me bleeding and beaten for that, and given Giovanni Guerra's violent reputation…well, I didn't know what to make of it.

"Sit down." He towered over me, reminding me just how weak I'd been against him only moments ago.

"I'd rather not." I rubbed at my neck where I could still feel the indentations of his fingers on my skin.

"It wasn't a request." His large hand landed on my shoulder, forcing me to sit on the edge of the mattress. "Stay."

"I'm not a dog."

"Then stop acting like a rabid stray."

Heat rushed over my face. "I thought…"

"You thought what?" The question felt like a threat dancing in the air between us, daring me to say the wrong thing. But I didn't have to. "I have plenty of willing women, princess. I don't need to force myself on little girls." His words shouldn't have annoyed me, but they did.

He was willing to marry someone he saw as nothing more than a child. For an alliance. For the Donato name. All the while, he had "plenty of willing women." Not like I ever expected anything else, but the bleak reality of my future if I failed to escape again spread out before me, cold and lonely, trapped. If I were going to be forced into marriage, it was definitely better not to have his attention, though.

Giovanni wrung out a cloth in the bowl of water, then held it a few inches from my face. "Are you going to behave, or shall I leave you to bleed everywhere?"

It was almost a kindness. Almost. And I didn't know what to do with that. He reached for the dressing on my head, tugging it away. I tried not to look at him, to ignore the gentle brush of his fingers on my skin, the same fingers that were stained by so much blood. The action of him caring for me was strangely intimate, and I wanted nothing of the sort with this man.

After a few seconds, I found myself staring, studying him. Veins roped his forearms and popped beneath tattooed skin as he wrung out the blood-stained cloth. The buttons of his shirt strained over his chest, and I couldn't help but admire the way the material lovingly caressed every muscle. He was too much, too perfect for violence and blood beneath his nails. But I'd heard the stories and witnessed first-hand just how ruthless he could be. There was a glaring sense of danger he elicited that tainted the air like the scent of death on the wind. This was a man even my uncle feared, and that was both thrilling and horrifying.

He finally applied a new dressing and took a step back, allowing me a breath of air that wasn't completely bathed in his scent. "There are men in the hall, the lobby, and the parking garage," he said as he moved toward the door. "Should you somehow make it past them, I own every inch of this city. You will be returned to me and locked in this penthouse. With me and the consequences of your actions." He cocked a brow, ice hardening in his eyes. "But go ahead and try me, princess. I might just enjoy those consequences."

I gaped at his back as he pulled open the door and left. And without him to distract me, the sense of claustrophobia closed around me instantly. It was just like being in the basement of my father's house, and I was every bit as trapped.

5

GIO

T he first gray light of dawn crept through the windows of my office. The city would soon stir to life, but this was my favorite time, when creatures of the night were melting back into the shadows, and normal, law-abiding citizens were yet to rise. My laptop sat on the desk in front of me, the camera feed showing all the rooms in the penthouse, but my attention was only on one. Emilia's slight form tossed and turned beneath the bedsheets, and I wondered what plagued her dreams. Was it me? Was I the monster under her bed? The thought brought a small smile to my lips. The girl was not what I had expected. She was innocent, yes, but she wore defiance like armor, wielding distrust as a weapon.

Every time I closed my eyes, I saw her on her knees with a gun to her head, and my temper spiked. The Outfit had tried to kill her. The circumstances mattered not, only that the bargain had already been struck. Emilia was mine. Mine to hunt, to punish, to take, and they tried to put her down. Worse, though, was the acceptance I saw when she had that gun to her head. She'd accepted death, and it troubled me, especially now I knew just how much fight she had. I reached up and ran my finger along one of the angry, raised lines her nails had carved into my throat. There weren't many hardened men who would dare to try to hurt me, but the hissing little kitten had.

Since taking over the day-to-day running of New York from Nero, I had to become harder, more ruthless, numb to certain atrocities. Morals I once had were now a mere whisper in the back of my mind because morals were idealistic. Emilia Donato was the image of idealism, though, young and innocent, and whatever sliver of conscience I had left was clawing at the cage I'd locked it in.

Dammit. My fist slammed into the desk, knuckles cracking with the force. She'd cost me four days hunting her down, and I was no closer to getting any product into the city. New York was already rife with rebellion without its supply. The officials I paid to look the other way would soon get twitchy when their streets filled with crime and those vying for power left trails of bodies.

Emilia Donato had cost me, and I wanted to wrap my hands around her pretty neck and choke her for it. My dick twitched at the thought.

I watched as she kicked the sheets away, revealing her long legs and my shirt still drowning her small body. A twisted sense of satisfaction rose at the sight of her in it, and my dick hardened when the material rode up her slim thighs, exposing white lace panties. A better man would look away, but I never pretended to be decent, and she was downright fucking *in*decent. I had every intention of ignoring my would-be bride, giving her my name and ring and locking her away in a safe place. But that was before she had run.

I hadn't anticipated her fierce defiance punching me in the gut every bit as hard as her curves punched me in the dick. She fought like she had nothing left to lose. And she was beautiful. All golden skin, wild chocolate curls, and a body that was made to be bent over something. Her eyes were the exact color of the Mediterranean Ocean at dusk, and in them lingered something so tragic, I wasn't sure if I wanted to fix her or break her entirely. Yes, I wanted to break her while she fought me like the savage little kitten she was, scratching and clawing until she drew blood. Until I had to choke her into submission again. I could almost feel her soft throat beneath my fingertips, the rush of her frantic pulse, part fear, part desire, part hate.

A better man would look away. A better man would let her go, but she'd made a fatal error; she'd drawn my attention. Emilia was a rose in full bloom, so blissfully unaware that her roots had been torn from the ground, but if I put a ring on her finger, would those thorns make me bleed? The thought excited me far more than it should.

So, what to do… Either way, she was now mine.

I was on the way to my Hampton House when Sergio Donato finally called me back. I'd already had his niece for over twelve hours.

"You must be busy, Donato. Hopefully, taking care of Patrick O'Hara," I said in the way of greeting.

"You took Emilia to New York?" His voice came through the car speakers, and I could picture the displeased frown on his withered face.

I noticed he didn't mention his dead men or the fact he'd ordered Emilia killed. I pulled onto the bridge, the very first pinks of the sunrise painting the surface of the water below. "Where else would I take her?"

"Chicago, of course." He hurried on before I could respond. "One of my underbosses has a daughter, Sofia. She's a widow but fertile. A good mafia wife."

I wanted to snap his neck. He pushed for this fucking marriage to seal an alliance, and I had agreed to marry some wilting little mafia princess who could be ignored and forgotten. Instead, he palmed off his unruly niece, probably hoping that whatever he'd threatened her with would keep her in check long enough to walk down the aisle. And now that she'd shown him up and failed to die in that motel room, he thought to swap her like faulty goods.

"No." My temper simmered below the surface until I was driving way over the speed limit. "Emilia is mine. Bought and paid for."

He scoffed. "Are you seriously telling me you still want to marry my niece after she ran and dishonored you?"

The Outfit with their honor and false morals... "I didn't want to marry her in the first place, Donato. And you don't really give a shit if I do. You want my political ties, my guns, and my coke. I have Emilia. Consider our alliance sealed."

There was a beat of silence. "You're right. I don't care what you do with her." Because he was a piece of shit. "But marriages have certain…benefits, and that is what you agreed to." He thought becoming family would offer him protection, but no one could protect him from me when I decided I was done with him. And there would come a time because the man was a snake.

"Well then, you should have chosen a bride who was actually willing." A smile pulled at my lips, the kind that usually prefaced someone's death. "Make no mistake, this 'alliance' is convenient to me, but don't become *in*convenient, Donato." I let the threat linger before he finally released a breath.

"Fine. She's yours. Marry her, fuck her, I don't care." I couldn't deny that I wanted to fuck her, but I wanted her begging and needy first. I shifted in the seat as my dick stirred at the thought. "Under one condition."

"You're in no position to make demands, Sergio."

"If and when you are done with her, you return her."

"Why?"

"She's still a Donato. I have another who petitioned for her hand before we struck our deal. If you do not want her…"

Then he'd sell her off like some broken broodmare to be used and bred. The thought made me want to burn the entire Outfit to the ground.

I would not be giving her back. Ever. "Done."

"Good. I would like my nephew returned to me as well."

Of course, he would. Who knew what kind of information we might extract from the boy.

"No. The guns will be with you tomorrow." I hung up. I didn't give a shit what he would like.

Sergio thought himself my equal, but he was a puppet to do my dirty work, his men foot soldiers in my war. The second he stepped out of line, I would crush him. It might be next week. It might be in a year. No amount of pretty little virgin pussy would protect him.

By the time I made it to the house, the sun had fully risen, and sweat dotted the back of my neck as I approached the front door. The house came with the job, and it was ostentatious as fuck, a brick mansion that spoke of old money. Tommy and some of my men stayed here, handling most of my business from within these walls.

A shiny black SUV sat in the middle of the driveway, and leaning against it, waiting for me, was Nero. He looked like a billboard advertising the damn car with his expensive suit and side swept dark hair.

I approached him, gravel crunching beneath my shoes. "You waiting on that call from *Vogue*?"

He snorted. "Don't be jealous, just because your fiancée ran away from your ugly ass."

I flipped him off, and he laughed as we walked into the house. The second we were inside, his demeanor changed. Nero was my best friend. We'd grown up together along with Tommy and Jackson. But in front of our men, he was simply the ruthless King of New York. His currency was blood, and his conscience was non-existent.

My shoes clicked over the polished hardwoods as we made our way into the kitchen, the scent of coffee and bacon greeting us. Tommy leaned against the breakfast bar, a mug of coffee in one hand and a half-eaten croissant in the other. The housekeeper, Louisa, was cooking eggs and bacon, feeding the guys sitting at the huge kitchen table. There was something soothing in the low buzz of conversation amongst my men, a sense of family, the only kind I'd known in the last decade. It made what I had to do so much worse.

A hush fell over the room, but not because of me. My power was absolute, except when Nero was in a room because fear trumped respect. They respected me, but even our men feared him as though he were the devil himself.

I'd invited all my capos here for a breakfast meeting because our situation was reaching a crisis point. It had been ten days and I was no closer to finding my rat. I'd stopped sending shipments because if you had a leak, you didn't keep sailing into open water.

Jackson sat at the head of the table and gave me an imperceptible nod of support. He was just as blood-thirsty to find this fucker as I was. All I knew was that it had to be one of the men in this room, and that pissed me off just as much as it hurt. Tommy followed me over to the table and took a seat. Nero and I remained standing.

I cleared my throat and waited as, one by one, the men at the table all fell silent and turned their attention toward me.

"We have a rat."

The silence that followed my statement was so profound, I could have heard a pin drop. I scanned each face for a reaction and knew the guys were, too.

"As you know, we've lost several shipments in Chicago. Some of which the details were known only to the people in this room."

Andrea, one of the older capos before Nero and I ever held power, shifted in his seat. "There's only one person here with Irish ties."

Tommy laughed, but I did not. "If you have something to say, Andrea, by all means, come out and say it."

The man swallowed heavily, his nervous gaze shifting to Nero before dropping to the table. Not so brave now.

"I didn't think so. The underbosses are not here because we suspect them." Tommy and Jackson were loyal to a fault. They were family. Brothers. I'd trust them with my life.

"One of you is a rat, and believe me when I say, I will find you. And when I do..."

Nero took a step closer to the table. "Come forward now and your families won't be harmed."

Andrea glared at him, which was foolish. "We don't touch women or children." Ah, the old Famiglia and their fucking ideals.

"This is not the old Famiglia," Nero sounded bored, probably because he'd heard this a thousand times. "I do not play by their rules. You know this." He rounded the table, shifting closer to Andrea. "You know well what I will do to your wife and children if you've betrayed me." He clapped a hand on the man's shoulder, squeezing hard enough that the older man winced. "Have you betrayed me, Andrea? Are you a filthy rat?"

"N-no," he stumbled, and Nero grinned, his expression totally fucking depraved.

Jesus, he played the mad man far too well. Not that it was really an act. I'd never actually let him kill innocent kids. The threat was powerful, though, because he'd done it before.

I cleared my throat. "I offer you the opportunity to come forward now and protect your families." I stared right at Andrea as I said it.

He sure had a lot to say on the subject, but that made me think it wasn't him. No, our rat would be one of the silent ones who couldn't look at me.

"You will not be afforded this opportunity again."

No one moved, every single man staring at the food in front of them like it was the most fascinating thing in the world, except Tommy, who was happily eating as though nothing were happening.

"How disappointing. Well then, you're free to go."

They scrambled away, leaving full plates in their wake.

I met Jackson's gaze at the end of the table. "Have them followed." A panicked rat would act blindly. We just had to wait and watch.

Nero left straight after the meeting, probably to resume dad duties. After breakfast, I pushed to my feet and glanced at Tommy. "I assume Renzo Donato is still alive."

He placed his coffee down. "Yeah. You going to keep him that way? He did kinda steal your girl."

"For now." Donato wanted the boy back, which meant he was useful. "Where is he?"

With a jerk of his head, he stood up and moved into the hallway. I followed him to the basement and past the interrogation room before he unlocked the door at the end of the dark corridor. It was a cell of sorts, used for holding prisoners between interrogations. We never used it, though, because Jackson always cracked them on the first go.

Renzo Donato was on a single bed in the windowless, cinderblock room. His skin was pale, dark hair matted to his forehead, and a blood bag attached to his arm. He looked like shit in the unique way that only a man who had brushed death could, but he was alive and conscious. He struggled to sit up, clutching his bandaged stomach.

"Where the fuck is my sister?" The words seemed to take considerable effort.

"She's safe." For now. The words hung in the air between us, unspoken but no less potent for their silence.

He glared at me. "Is that where you get your kicks? Forcing yourself on unwilling girls?"

In my periphery, Tommy straightened away from the wall. "I suggest you shut up before he decides he doesn't need you alive."

"My marriage to your sister was your uncle's stipulation, not mine. I find it to be... an ineffective way of sealing alliances."

His brows furrowed. "Then don't do it. Just let her go. Emilia isn't like us. She's..." His gaze dropped to the blanket over his legs. "She deserves better." The boy was entrenched in the mafia, an enforcer for his father at the tender age of twenty-four, and yet he'd risked it all to help her run. Even now, in the hands of a potential enemy, he pled for her freedom. Interesting. Renzo Donato was not what I expected.

"As touching as your ideals are, an alliance with your family is convenient to me. I don't like to sully myself with Chicago." I let a cold smirk wash over my face. "And let's be honest, having Emilia in my bed is no hardship."

His jaw ticced, fists balling against the sheets. "You're a piece of shit."

I knew exactly what he was thinking, and I didn't correct him. Let him think I was the monster in his pretty little sister's story. "Of course, if you were to give me something else… a bargaining chip—"

"You think I'm going to sell out my family?" He huffed a painful-sounding laugh. "To you of all people."

I smiled, placing a hand on my chest. "I'm hurt."

"You have no fucking honor," he snarled. "You don't deserve my sister."

My temper threatened to spike as he spoke of honor when he came from a nest of vipers. "Oh, and your honorable family who tried to kill her does?"

His face washed even paler.

"That's what I thought." I turned away from him and walked out of the room.

It was a seed of dissent, planted and waiting to grow. He loved his sister, and no emotion was so easily exploited or manipulated as love. The Outfit was useful to me for now, but information was currency, and when dealing with men like Sergio Donato, I always liked to keep the key to their destruction in my back pocket. I wouldn't waste the opportunity to gather such information, especially when Renzo would do anything for his sweet little sister.

6

EMILIA

I'd been in this room for at least a day, though without a window, it was impossible to know exactly. All I had to go on were those screens changing from a starry night sky over the Nevada desert to a sunrise on a beach, then a scene of the mountains, and finally a sunset somewhere in Asia, before returning to night again. That was more than I'd ever had in the basement, and if I tried hard, I could almost pretend those screens were an actual window. It kept the nagging sense of panic at bay for a little while.

Despite being in this room with nothing to do but sleep or stare at the wall, I was exhausted. Every time I closed my eyes, nightmares plagued me, shadowy figures trying to kill me, and my brother bleeding out, dying. My only distraction from the four walls pressing in on me was a pen and notebook I'd found in the nightstand. I sat cross-legged on the bed, shading a bloody heart clutched in a fist. Drawing something I always had in the basement. That and reading, because notepads, books, and pencils were all my father allowed me to have down there. I'd found a certain solace in it, though, a way to express myself in a world where emotions were unwelcome.

I paused as footsteps approached my door. It swung open with a bang, and I scrambled off the bed. Giovanni smirked, clearly amused by my skittish state, before leaning against the doorframe. Shirtless. Very shirtless and clearly fresh from a workout. My cheeks burned as I took in the sheen of sweat on his chest. I had the insane urge to touch the defined planes, to catch that bead of sweat rolling between his pecs. I told myself to look at the floor, the ceiling, anything. *Anywhere.* But my gaze trailed down a body that was every bit as perfect as his face. Giovanni Guerra was a sinful lure, all golden skin and tattoos. That deep *V* that dropped into the waistband of his workout shorts…

He made a suit look good, but this… yeah, this was better. No, worse. Of all the issues I thought I might experience when I was promised to this man, being attracted to him was not one of them. In that moment, I loathed myself for feeling even an inkling of lust toward him. If I needed confirmation that the man was a monster, I had it because only the devil could be that beautiful.

His gaze swept over me unapologetically, and my arms folded over my chest, trying to hide myself, even though I'd just been doing the same thing. But I wasn't parading around half-naked.

"You look like shit," he finally said, dragging his hand through dark, unruly curls.

"Thanks. Getting pistol-whipped, then kidnapped, and shot by an asshole will do that for you." I expected that to earn me some pain, but he ignored me.

"There's food in the kitchen. Go eat."

It wasn't a suggestion, more like a command, but I wasn't one of his damn soldiers. "No."

His jaw clenched, his fists tightening at his sides. "Emilia—" he growled out my name like a curse, and I cut him off.

"Is my brother alive?"

His angry gaze settled over me as if deliberating how cruel he wanted to be today. "If I tell you, will you go eat?"

Why the hell did he care if I ate or not? I nodded anyway, eager for any news of Renzo.

"Yes, he is alive."

"Where is he?"

That seemed to be the limits of his kindness, though. "As I said before, worry about yourself, princess."

I rounded the bed, only stopping when I was a couple of feet away from him. "What are you going to do, Giovanni? Kill me?"

No, worse, he was going to marry me. I shouldn't have pushed him, but the unfairness of it all, the hopelessness, drove me past rational and right into reckless territory. Maybe in some twisted corner of my mind, I wanted his cruelty because that was what I expected, what I knew. And I needed familiar ground because I was so far out of my comfort zone.

A small smile curled the corner of his lips. "Why would I kill you, piccola?"

It felt like a trick question. One that had me swallowing any sharp retort I might have had. He stepped to the side as though gesturing for me to move past him. And suddenly, the room that had felt like a prison cell now felt like a haven.

"I'm not hungry." My stomach growled out a betrayal, but I just grabbed the door, ready to slam it in his face.

His foot pressed against the wood before I could, fingers gripping the frame on both sides as though he were physically holding himself back. His biceps strained with the movement, and that sapphire gaze collided with mine, hard and filled with promises of violence.

"You have five minutes to get out here." This guy really thought I'd just jump through his hoops.

"No."

"You made a deal. I told you your brother's alive. Of course, that could always change…."

I jabbed a finger into his very unforgiving chest. "Are you threatening Renzo's life just because I won't do what you say?"

He pressed into my touch, and I was caught somewhere between hate and the urge to push my entire palm to his warm skin. "Are you breaking your word?"

I yanked away my hand, eyes raking his body with feigned disgust. "No. I'll eat. Just not now, and certainly not with you."

I swear I saw the corner of his mouth twitch, but it was gone in an instant. He stepped back into the hall, straightening to his full height.

"Don't be a brat, Emilia."

A brat? I was a brat because I wanted my freedom? To be treated like a person and not cattle at market….

My temper rose like an angry viper, and I gripped the door. "Fuck you, Giovanni." I slammed it in his face and stood there, pulse hammering in anticipation because I fully expected him to smash it down. To come in here and punish me, hurt me, bend me to his will. Instead, I heard his retreating footsteps and then silence. I didn't know what to do with that. I'd only known the man for a day, but he was unpredictable, and I didn't like unpredictable.

As much as the rebellious little voice in my head told me to dig in my heels, to fight him every step of the way to that damn altar, I was hungry. And I did really want out of this damn room. I glanced down at his T-shirt that barely covered me and wished I had some actual clothes, some armor against him. Everything I'd been wearing when he had caught me was covered in blood, my jeans cut up.

My stomach growled again, reminding me that I hadn't eaten since Renzo had stopped for fast food outside that shitty little town. On a deep breath, I pulled open the door and stepped out into the empty hallway. The wooden floor was cold beneath my bare feet as I made my way toward the living area, each careful footstep like a gunshot in the silence of the apartment.

When I reached the end of the hall, I lingered there like a stray cat, ensuring no one was around before coming out for scraps. The only illumination in the penthouse came from some strip lighting in the kitchen and the perpetual glow of the city below. Maybe Giovanni had left. Surely, he had better things to do than babysit me, mafia bad-guy shit to do. I glanced at the front door, the glossy black so inconspicuous. I knew it would be locked but couldn't help myself.

I tried the handle. Locked and without any obvious keyhole, just the handle and what looked like a scanner for a key card. Okay, so it seemed like he was gone and I was alone. This was an opportunity. My stomach clenched again. Food first. Then escape. The contents of the refrigerator were meager, though it wasn't like I actually had a clue how to make anything. In reality, cereal was about the extent of my skills. I decided to attempt a grilled cheese because how hard could it be? Even Renzo managed it. The thought of my brother had my chest tightening with guilt. I couldn't even help myself right now, so how would I help him? Not like I could appeal to Giovanni's heart. The man clearly didn't have one.

I shoved my bread and cheese concoction into the oven under the burner, then uncorked a bottle of wine that was in the refrigerator and poured it into a mug because I couldn't reach the glasses. My mother's aghast face popped into my head. Come to think of it, drinking wine from a mug would be more horrifying to her than the fact I was being held prisoner and forced to marry against my will. She'd say I was lucky to be engaged to a man as handsome as him. Because you know, I had no say in who I married, so I should at least be grateful he was pretty. God, I hated my whole family. Except for Renzo and maybe Luca sometimes.

It was said you could tell a lot about a person from their space, and I knew nothing about Giovanni Guerra other than his fearsome reputation.

Uplighting flickered to life along the floor when I strolled into the living room. A corner sofa sat in front of a fire flickering behind a pane of glass, and a crystal chandelier reflected little spots of light through the darkness like glitter. The entire apartment was beautiful, but much like my parents' house, it felt unlived in, all for show. It told me nothing other than the fact that he probably wasn't here a lot.

I moved to the massive windows and pressed my palm against the cool glass, taking in the city that stretched beyond me like a mirage I couldn't quite touch. From here, New York was a sea of stars dancing in a black ocean. I'd always loved the vastness of Lake Michigan, the way it stretched to the horizon endlessly. I loved the sandy shores and the woods that always smelled of damp earth and pine, where I could immerse myself so entirely that I could almost pretend not a soul existed in the world except me. I missed it, but I was also mesmerized by the chaotic nature of this place.

The high-pitched shrieking of the fire alarm cut through my thoughts. Shit. I rushed to the kitchen to see smoke billowing around the seal of the oven door, and I panicked. There was a fire, I was locked in this damn place, and I had no idea what to do. I debated throwing water at the door when the shrieking cut off. Giovanni's sudden presence startled me in the deafening silence. He brushed past me and turned off the oven before opening a sliding door that led to a balcony. Right. Probably should have turned off the oven, at least.

Smoke billowed out into the night air before he turned around, thick arms folded over his chest as a frown marred his face. At least he had on a shirt now, though the material was plastered to his biceps in a really distracting way. "Your tantrum need not extend to burning down my apartment."

"If only I could. Preferably with you in it."

There was that twitch of his lip again. He opened the oven and wafted away the huge cloud of smoke that came out, then stared at the charred remains of my sandwich. Low flames still flickered pitifully in the grill pan, and a tiny sound huffed past his lips that could almost be taken for a laugh. "How did you burn a sandwich?"

"I don't know how to cook." My stomach let out another growl, and I silenced it with a heavy swig of wine.

At this rate, I was going to be drunk and hungry.

"That's not cooking."

"It required an oven."

He cocked a brow. "Your kitchen rights are revoked."

"Oh, look at that. Right along with my human rights." I offered him a saccharine smile and opened the fridge, taking the bottle of wine on pure principle. Then I headed toward my room/jail cell. I made it three steps before a large hand clamped around the back of my neck, and I froze like prey in the jaws of a lion. I was yanked back until every inch of his hard body pressed against me. My brain stuttered to a halt, the panicked beat of my pulse hammering in my ears.

I tried to remain calm, to think, but he loomed over me, around me, ensnaring me. Warm breath trickled over my neck, and it felt like a dangerous precursor to those sharp teeth tearing me apart. His woodsy, minty scent mixed with the smoke in the air as his thumb swept just below my ear in a strangely soothing gesture. The warmth of his body bled into me like a furnace on a cold night, and I shivered in his hold, fear slowly giving way to a tentative kind of curiosity.

It unfurled within me like some dormant beast I'd never been aware of before now. An indignant little voice screamed that there was no room for curiosity here, no matter how much electricity skittered over my skin at that soft sweep of his thumb. He suddenly felt like something dangerous yet alluringly safe. A weapon that could be used for or against me. A weapon that I was leaning into as though I were already drunk.

He forced my head to the right, exposing the side of my neck like he might very well tear out my jugular. Instead, his lips brushed my racing pulse in a featherlight caress, and that was worse. So much worse, because instead of him being the enemy, my own body became my adversary. I couldn't breathe, couldn't move, couldn't think beyond the soft scratch of his stubble on my over-sensitized skin.

"That is a bottle of Montrachet." Every rough syllable of his voice dragged over my senses.

He'd captured me, shot me, threatened to hurt me. And now he played me like a puppet on strings, and I hated him for it almost as much as I hated myself for reacting in any way. I was no one's puppet.

Yanking out of his hold, I turned to face him. I had to tilt back my chin to look up at him, and this close, he was even more beautiful. Honeyed poison.

One dark brow cocked over cold eyes, daring the mouse to snap at the cat. "And you're drinking it out of a mug."

I placed the wine bottle to my lips and tipped it back with a heavy slosh, hoping that if I feigned enough courage, it would become real. "Better?"

Rough fingers swept over my cheek so gently, it was unnerving. That touch said he could destroy me if he wanted to and he wouldn't even need violence.

"And I thought you'd be a perfectly cowed, true Outfit princess." He tsked.

"You wouldn't have agreed to marry me if you knew the truth, would you?" I took another swig from the bottle and smiled, though it was a vicious, resentful thing. "My uncle seems to know you like your women 'cowed' and on their knees, though."

And Uncle Sergio had sold him a lie.

A wicked smirk crossed Giovanni's lips before his hand clamped around my throat. He wrenched me up against him, and the thready note of fear rattled through my lungs, but it was laced with a heady kind of thrill at the sense of danger that surrounded him so effortlessly. I was losing my damn mind.

"You're right about one thing, piccola." His voice was a seductive rumble that caressed my already fraught senses. "I do like a woman on her knees."

My pulse thrummed erratically, and I knew he could probably feel it, probably mistook it for fear and liked it.

He leaned in, and I froze as his lips brushed my cheek, dragging a burning trail to my ear. "But I like her there wet and begging." His teeth scraped my ear. "Right before I fuck her throat."

My face burned, and I sucked in a ragged breath. "Well then, it seems my uncle screwed us both because neither of us will be getting what we want." My voice wavered slightly, and I knew he heard it. I planted my knuckles that were fisted around the wine bottle against his chest, shoving away from him with as much strength as I could muster. Not enough to force him to let go of me, but he did.

That smirk remained on his lips as calloused fingers brushed mine, gripping the bottle of wine. I let go like it was on fire, then turned and practically ran to my room. I needed to get away from him.

7

GIO

J ackson and I stepped off the elevator and into the morning bustle of the Chicago DA's office. The scent of coffee and stuffy air conditioning filled the space. It was the smell of people grinding through life.

The attention we drew as we passed through the rows of cubicles was not unwanted because the man I was here to see —well, the last thing he wanted was to be seen with me. Such was the two-faced nature of my world. People liked dirty money, but not the dirty consequences that came with it. I approached the district attorney's office, and his secretary, Diana, looked up from her desk. The young woman's gaze met mine, and a slight blush colored her cheeks as she nodded, making no move to stop me. I knew the DA was alone because I paid her to report his movements.

When I swung open the door, Hector Langford jumped behind his glass desk, opening his mouth before snapping it shut again.

"Mr. Guerra. What are you doing here? I could have met you—"

"Ah, Hector, you know as well as I do that I'm here to make a point."

Jackson shut the door and placed his back to it, thick arms folding over an even thicker chest. He was a figurative wall trapping Hector in this office—with me. That was a position few men wanted to find themselves in.

I moved over to the window and took in the view of Chicago sprawled beyond the windows. The city lacked the charm of my home, but I could admit there was a certain beauty in the glittering of Lake Michigan in the distance. I turned around, watching as the DA swallowed heavily.

Hector Langford was a short man, his gut straining against the buttons of a suit that had probably fit him at one time. He shifted in his chair, wide eyes darting toward the office door as though he was debating trying to make a run for it. Maybe he thought he could get through Jackson, but I suspected he was more concerned about someone walking in here. It wouldn't do for him to be seen with someone like me. Not that anyone could ever pin me for criminal activity, but whispers traveled like the wind, bouncing from city to city. My reputation was engraved into the bloody history of Chicago.

"I got your message, but I can't do what you're asking," he hissed under his breath, tugging at the collar of his shirt.

I reveled in his discomfort. "You know, Hector, I'm a busy man. But I came here in person to speak with you."

"I can't—"

I unfastened the button of my jacket, allowing it to fall open and reveal the leather chest holster and pistol strapped beneath my arm. "You can, and you will."

The man's brows crumpled, and he glared at me. "Or what? I'm the DA. You're not going to kill me in my own office." He tried to sound confident, but the slight waver in his voice combined with the sweat dotting his brow told me otherwise. "I only have to say the word and all your shipments would be seized. I could fuck you over, too, Guerra."

I let out a sigh. "What a shame. You know, I thought you might have taken heed of your predecessor's demise." I smiled, and he blanched.

The unfortunate former DA had become entwined with "local gangs" and had been tortured and hung from the Canal Street Bridge, according to reports.

"But you're right. If I kill you, I have to start all over again with a new DA. And what if he's not a dirty, greedy bastard who can be bought like you?"

Jackson laughed.

"Last chance, Hector. What will it be?"

The man's jaw ticced, his face turning an ugly shade of red. "No," he said, like a defiant, petulant child.

A long sigh came from behind me, and Jackson shook his head as he moved beside me and held out his phone.

A video call was already connected to one of his soldiers, the man waiting on my cue. "Just remember, I gave you the chance to be reasonable, Hector, and you pushed me." I took the phone and turned the screen so he could see it, right before the soldier panned the camera around to show a children's play park. Kids ran around, so blissful in their innocence. Hector's children played with their nanny, the young woman smiling and pushing his son on the swings, so unaware of the danger lurking nearby in the form of one of my men.

I watched the sheer horror play over Hector's features. Perfect. He tugged at his tie, face paling to a sickly shade of gray. And I knew he suddenly realized that in his world, he held a degree of power but we were not the same. In my world, I was absolute, and I would do things without blinking that he wouldn't even consider. And the second he took my money? Well, that set him firmly in my world, with my boot on his fucking neck. This was his introduction to said boot.

"No. They're just children." He shook his head, unable to tear his gaze from the camera. "Please."

"Tsk, tsk." I pulled an envelope from the inside pocket of my jacket and slid it in front of him. "Children are a weakness, are they not? So innocent." And if he didn't want to put them at risk, then he never should have sold his soul to me.

"You're disgusting," he spat.

I cut the call before handing the phone back to Jackson. "You didn't seem to think so when you were taking my money. Now, inside that envelope is a ten grand bonus and a list of mob shipments that will be arriving in Chicago over the next two weeks."

They might have a rat in my ranks, but buying one in theirs hadn't proved too difficult. I had offered an exorbitant amount of money. Enough to risk death, apparently.

Hector picked up the envelope, swallowing heavily. "How do you know when their shipments are arriving?"

"The same way I knew you were alone in your office this morning and your children were at the park." I pushed to my feet. "I have people everywhere, Mr. Langford." His nanny, his secretary. People were predictable, driven by money over loyalty. "You will open a case against Patrick O'Hara and make his life very difficult. Seize their shipments, arrest their soldiers, close down his legal businesses. Pick them apart."

He glanced down at his desk, his expression becoming pinched. "O'Hara will kill me," he whispered.

"Well, they say a man will die for his children."

He looked like he was planning his own funeral as I turned and left the office. I would have men watch Hector's house and his children in case the mob thought to target them. I might make threats, but I wouldn't actually hurt them. Despite my bloody reputation, children and innocents were my line. All men had to have one, lest we become nothing more than beasts. Nero was the one with no such line, and his reputation bled into mine until everyone associated with us was a demon in someone's eyes. However, years as his second had taught me one thing; when it comes to those they love, people aren't prepared to take a chance that the threat may not be real.

Jackson and I were in the car before I spoke again.

"I'm going to arrange a meeting with the Pérez brothers," I said.

He pulled out of the parking garage, fingers tightening perceptibly on the steering wheel. "Now we're bypassing Rafe and getting coke from those shady little shits?"

"Just one shipment. I can't trust Chicago right now with our fucking rat." I'd gotten one shipment through in the last week by telling no one but the guys moving it, but two others had been taken with the same tactic. I couldn't afford to play Russian roulette with hundreds of thousands of dollars worth of product. Rafael might well bitch, but he'd bitch a whole lot more when I couldn't pay him.

"You know Rafe won't ship elsewhere, either."

Because the cartel leader had some weird little bubble of FBI protection in Chicago. Hence why we never lost product and why Sergio Donato was so keen to get coke from us. Between whoever Rafe had bought off and all the people in my pocket, we were untouchable. At least from anyone on the legal side of things. The mob would soon learn exactly how untouchable we were.

"Let's go pay the councilman a visit." I was going to wrap Patrick O'Hara up in so much red tape, he wouldn't be able to shit without someone breathing down his neck. Licenses, planning applications, business rates, the IRS...I would drown his legal stuff while The Outfit hit their warehouses and killed their soldiers. "Then I have a meeting with Roberto Donato."

"We could just handle this all ourselves, you know. We don't need the fucking Outfit."

"We're above fighting in the streets like petty criminals, Jackson."

"Speak for yourself," he mumbled. "I'd happily gut Sergio Donato and the fucking mob. Still can't believe he tried to kill his own niece." He shook his head, and if Jackson thought something was screwed up, it was bad.

Rage simmered through my veins, but I kept a handle on it. "His time will come."

At the mention of Emilia, I took out my phone and pulled up the feed for the cameras in my apartment. It had become almost habitual over the last forty-eight hours since she'd been in my space. I was rarely there and had men guarding the penthouse and the building, but I still kept checking. I told myself it was to make sure she didn't escape, but it was more than that, some twisted curiosity she'd ignited in me.

The screen showed her walking into her room from the bathroom, a towel wrapped around her body. When she dropped it and gifted me a view of her bare back and ass, my dick hardened against my fly. Fuck. My teeth ground together, and I turned the phone screen down in my lap. Not because I was decent but because I needed to focus. Clearing my throat, I looked at Jackson.

"We just need to wait for Paddy O'Hara's house to catch fire." My voice had a slight rasp that I couldn't quite cover. "Contact the Pérez brothers and organize a meeting. The last thing we need is a war on our *own* turf because we can't supply."

I turned my phone over again and found Emilia's room empty. I thought she might be in the bathroom, where I wasn't perverse enough to have a camera. A choice I was regretting right now. I could imagine how good she'd look in the shower, water cascading over those perfect curves. I switched cameras and found her in the kitchen. My shirt once again drowned her body and left her legs bare. The bandage on her thigh peeked out from beneath the material, reminding me that she was a bird—whose wings I had personally clipped—trapped in my cage.

She crept through the space like a flighty prey animal, limping slightly. I couldn't deny that I wanted to chase her, take her, taste her. She opened a kitchen drawer and took something out. A knife? Then closed it and darted back to her room. I couldn't help but smile. Was she going to try to kill me? I wouldn't put it past her.

Emilia Donato did not know how to submit. She sure as hell wasn't willing to marry some guy her daddy, or more specifically her uncle, had picked out for her. I'd never bought into the mafia tradition of arranged marriages and only agreed for a quick fix to an irritating problem. But she was no longer the annoying consequence of an Outfit alliance. Rather, the alliance was the cherry on top, and she was the best sundae I was ever going to taste.

I couldn't pinpoint exactly when it had changed, maybe the very second I'd heard that she'd run. It was unexpected, impulsive, and defiant. And despite the inconvenience of it, she had me intrigued right then. Who was this girl who would defy the leaders of two mafias? The moment I looked into those pretty eyes of hers and saw nothing but pure venom shining back at me, her fate was sealed. And when I felt the erratic thrum of her pulse beneath my lips, it was set in stone. She could run, and I would chase her to the ends of the Earth on pure principle. Her submission would be a brutal battle of will and lust, and the thought made my cock painfully hard. In the space of a week,

Emilia Donato had become an obsession, and I *would* have her.

Jackson glanced at the phone in my hand, and I didn't even care if he saw me stalking her. "Are you really going to force a girl who ran away from you, to marry you, just to appease Sergio Donato?"

"No."

He snorted. "Thought not. You're too moral, Gio." Only he or Nero would possibly ever say that, and only because they were such psychopaths. I was many things, but least of all, moral.

"You know, you could always just give her back. Remove the issue." He glanced at my screen again, probably sensing the distraction she absolutely was. "I doubt they'll actually kill her. They'll just marry her off to some fuck who's less concerned with her willingness."

The thought of them killing her simply because she wouldn't be their puppet bothered me, but another guy having her … that sent me over the edge.

"She's not going back." I wasn't sure what I was doing with her. The only thing I did know—she was mine. By the time I was done with Emilia Donato, she'd be begging me to keep her.

8

EMILIA

Turned out, Giovanni was rarely here, and if the pile of take-out bags outside my bedroom door was anything to go by, one of his men was delivering food regularly. Like a neighbor feeding the cat. Well, I didn't want Giovanni's damn food, so he could go screw himself.

The benefit of his absence was that I had ample opportunity to find an escape. Except there was none. The front door was locked, of course, with no keyhole to even attempt to pick. No fire exit and I didn't have wings, so I wasn't jumping off a balcony. What I did find, however, was a door that led to a set of stairs. With a paperclip stolen from Giovanni's office, I picked the lock at the top and found a rooftop terrace.

The view was breathtaking, with the city sprawled on one side and Central Park on the other. A cool breeze tinged with the briny scent of the ocean tugged at my hair as I took in the patio furniture and a bar in the corner. Giovanni really didn't strike me as the socializing or relaxing type, and I wondered if that door was ever unlocked.

I retrieved another bottle of his fancy wine and collapsed onto the rattan sofa, breathing in the fresh air as though it wasn't tainted by exhaust fumes from the city far below.

The lake house was a cage, and I'd spent more nights than I cared to remember in the basement, but the lake and woods were always there to suck me into their wild embrace whenever my father decided I'd served my sentence. I craved the wilderness now, but it was nowhere to be seen in this concrete jungle.

I lay down, taking in the deep navy of the night sky, scattered with stars. That was where I remained, drinking wine and waiting for some kind of master escape plan to hit me.

The moon was high in the sky when the door to the roof banged open so hard the hinges groaned in protest. Giovanni was like a rolling storm, his presence apparent long before I ever heard the first rumble of thunder. Power and the promise of violence brushed over my skin like static.

"What are you doing up here?" His voice was calm, but I knew that was a façade.

My pulse jumped, and in a sick way, I liked it. The adrenaline he ignited in me was like a shot of heroin in my veins, cutting through the darkness that surrounded me. "What does it look like, Giovanni?" I lifted the bottle of wine.

His shadow fell over me, his energy as choking as the hand he'd clasped around my throat a couple of nights ago. "*How* did you get up here?"

I sat up and swung my legs to the side until my feet touched the ground and my bare knees brushed the soft material of his suit pants. "Picked the lock."

He lifted a brow. "You picked. The. Lock?"

Renzo had taught me to pick a lock when I was ten. I almost smiled at the memory of Renzo, Chiara, and me breaking out and camping in the woods until my father's men had found us. "You aren't the first man to try to lock me up."

There was a beat of silence where his gaze swept the length of me. "Picking locks, going into my room…"

I glanced down at the shirt I'd stolen from his closet earlier.

"Tell me, Emilia, are you brave or just stupid?"

I smoothed a hand down the front of the black buttoned shirt, and his eyes tracked the movement like a hawk. I pushed to my feet, not that it brought us level or made him any less intimidating. It did, however, bring me flush against him, the couch behind my knees, trapping me. "It looks better on me anyway." That was an absolute lie because Giovanni was wearing an identical black shirt, and it clung to him like a jilted lover who couldn't let go.

He leaned in close, one finger brushing the collar before following the edge of the material down my chest, sending goose bumps skittering over my skin. "You're right." His voice was a sensual caress dragging over nerve endings without mercy. "It does."

In an instant, my body was burning, craving him like the traitor it was, like the toxic drug *he* was, and I hated it. Hated him. Hated myself.

My hand landed on his pec, fingers curling into his shirt as though I could dig them into his heart and pry it from his chest. His palm spanned the small of my back, pinning me against him.

"You know if you're going to hold me captive in this apartment, you could at least give me clothes."

His lips pulled up on one side. "And why would I do that when mine look so good on you?" Did he think this was some kind of game?

My temper spiked. "Are you just going to keep me locked up like some half-dressed little pet indefinitely?"

"For now."

Until he could drag me down the aisle. My chest tightened at the thought, and I tried to push away from him, but he wouldn't let me go. "You know, I don't want to marry you. I'd rather jump off this fucking building."

"Would you really?"

"Yes."

"Okay." He gripped my waist and lifted me, and my thighs instinctively clamped around his hips. "Let's test that theory, shall we?" He moved, and my entire body tensed when he set me on the edge of the glass railing that surrounded the rooftop.

"What are you doing?" I breathed, holding onto him tightly. Wind ripped at my hair, reminding me just how high we were. My heart jumped into my throat, knowing the sheer drop that lay behind me. Survival instincts seized my mind, and I clung to Gio like a baby monkey.

A smile played over his lips. "Do you trust me, piccola?" Not even slightly. "Do you think I'd let you fall?"

Adrenaline slammed through my veins like a freight train because I was scared, because I was more alive this close to death than I'd ever been.

"Do you think I'd let you die?" he breathed.

My arms wound around his neck, and he touched his forehead to mine, his warm breath washing over my lips. He could have let me die in that motel room, and he hadn't, but that didn't mean I trusted him or that I even wanted to. A blissful rush hammered against my temples, the night sky spinning around us, driving a familiar sense of recklessness.

"You don't own me, Giovanni, and you never will."

With that, I let go of him and leaned back. My weight teetered for a split second, and I half expected the wind to rush up around me, but deep down, I always knew he would catch me. His arm wrapped around my waist, a hand on the back of my neck, wrenching me up, then off the railing and against his chest. My feet hit the ground, limbs shaking.

Giovanni clutched me to him like a lover, my racing pulse drowning out everything as his lips brushed my cheek. "Defiant to the very end, Emilia, and *that* is why I want you. You sealed your fate the second you were brave enough to run. And now you're mine."

"I just tried to throw myself off a building to escape you."

He huffed a laugh. "But you always knew I would catch you, didn't you, princess? Deep down, you trust me. Deep down, you know I'll protect you...and kill for you." Like he had in that motel room.

Did I trust him? It didn't matter. I'd never play into Sergio's hands, never be their pawn. "Trust you, hate you," I shrugged. "It doesn't matter. I could love you, and I would still always fight you, Giovanni." Even as those words left my mouth, my body gravitated toward him, like an invisible thread suddenly bound us.

His nose traced the side of my throat on a groan. "I know. That's what makes you so perfect."

He straightened to his full height, and my heart hiccupped in my chest. I hated him, wanted to fight him until my last damn breath, but I saw how much he wanted me, beyond a simple family name. He was chasing, but the chase only lasted long enough that the predator either made the kill or lost interest. My hand in marriage was the only leverage I had here, and his wanting me was my only advantage. Maybe I could use that… He stepped away from me, and the cool breeze rushed in between us.

"Is my brother really alive?" I blurted, an idea forming in my mind.

He frowned. "I don't lie."

"Then send him home," I stammered, and Giovanni stilled. "Send Renzo home and I'll marry you willingly." My heartbeat threatened to choke me as I held my breath. This was all I had. The only card I could play, and I'd toss it into the ring for my brother.

Giovanni's jaw ticced. "No."

I frowned. "What? I thought that's what—"

"No."

"You want me on my knees begging, Giovanni? Is that it?"

He simply stared back at me. *I do like a woman on her knees.* I swallowed every ounce of pride I had as my bare knees met the cold patio slabs.

"Is this what you want? The girl you bought kneeling like a submissive little slave?" I spat the venomous words at him.

Rough fingers threaded through my hair, wrenching me flush to his thigh. The hard outline of his dick pressed to my cheek, and I gritted my teeth. He groaned, then forced me to look up at him.

"There is not a submissive bone in your body, Emilia, but fuck, you look good down there." He stepped back, releasing a long breath as his fists clenched at his sides. "Get up."

I did, and he reached out, tracing his knuckles over my jaw.

"When you agree to marry me, it won't be for your fucking brother. I want submission, not sacrifice." His thick thigh forced my legs apart until I was practically straddling him, the soft material of his pants caressing my skin. "And the next time you get on your knees like that, you will be willingly choking on my dick, princess." Never.

He stepped back so suddenly that I swayed on the spot. My heart beat an erratic tune in my chest, fear and that twisted sense of curiosity threading through my veins. I needed to find a way to escape him because Giovanni Guerra had the ability to make me weak.

———

It was the next afternoon when a knock came at my bedroom door. That in itself was weird because Giovanni's men never came in here, and he didn't knock; he just walked in. Still, I ignored it and kept dragging the pencil over the page. Of course, Giovanni's version of boundaries only lasted so long and he walked right in.

"Fuck off—"

He tossed a phone onto the bed and walked out without a word. I frowned down at the device and scooped it up. The red-haired guy who had helped kidnap me and threatened my brother was on the screen, his smile warm and inviting in a way that annoyed me.

"Hey, sweetheart. I'm Tommy, by the way. Didn't get a chance to introduce myself before."

"What—" The image blurred, and then it was Renzo's face filling the screen. I choked on a sob at the sight of him. "Renzo?"

My brother looked tired and pale but otherwise seemed okay. "Emi." His smile was like a fire when I'd been out in the freezing cold for days. "Are you okay? Did he hurt you?" he asked, his voice shaking slightly.

I shook my head. "I'm fine. Captive, but…fine. Are you okay?"

He raked a hand through his mop of dark curls. "Yeah, the bullet wound is healing."

"Good, that's…that's good." I tried and failed to blink away tears, and Renzo frowned.

"Don't cry, Emi. I'll get us out of this." Of course, he would say that, but his situation was worse than mine. He'd nearly died, and Giovanni Guerra didn't want in his pants.

His expression turned hard, jaw clenching. "When is the wedding?"

"I… don't know yet." I wasn't going to mention the fact that I had tried to barter for his freedom and was turned down. *I want submission, not sacrifice.* Giovanni had to know I'd never submit, though. "I have some time."

"If you don't marry him, then he'll have to send you back. Sergio—"

"I know. I know, Ren."

My brother knew what awaited me in Chicago. Renzo loved me, but I was pretty sure he'd rather I married Satan himself than go anywhere near Matteo Romano. That man was evil incarnate, and he'd already stolen too much from us.

"Stefano tried to kill you. I can't believe Dad would sign off on that. It's fucked up."

"It was Matteo," I whispered.

Renzo growled, pinching the bridge of his nose and turning his head away as though he were too ashamed to even look at me. "What Uncle Sergio did to you, to Chiara, is fucking wrong, Emi." He shook his head, his expression crumpling. "And one day, I promise you, I will kill him for it."

I believed him. I truly did.

"But until then, if you get the chance, you run. Get as far away from all this shit as you can. Because if you don't, you're going to end up married to one of them, and you'll never escape." Like Chiara, who'd only had one way out.

"But what about you?"

"I'll be fine. If Giovanni Guerra wanted me dead, I'd be dead. Without you, he'll need me as leverage even more. He obviously needs The Outfit for something."

If I ran, Renzo could still be safe… "I'll be fine; better if I knew you were away from all this. I don't want him using me against you."

I heard the click of what sounded like a door opening, followed by a murmured voice in the background before Renzo frowned.

"I have to go, Emi, but I love you. Do what I told you. Please."

Tears pricked my eyes. "I love you." Then the call cut off.

I sat there, staring at the home screen of the phone for a moment, tears tracking down my cheeks. That was how Giovanni found me when he walked in with a bowl in hand— sitting on the bed, staring blankly at his phone. The smell of herbs and cheese wafted over me as he placed the food on the nightstand. I pushed to my feet and handed him the phone.

"Thank you," I said hoarsely. "For letting me talk to him."

His fingers brushed mine as he took it, and I suddenly felt so utterly deprived of affection. I wanted to hug Renzo so badly.

"I didn't lie to you." It seemed important to him that I knew it. As awful as Giovanni Guerra might be, he wasn't a liar. He reached out and swiped a tear from my cheek. "You're so pretty when you cry, piccola." The words were dark, but they settled in my chest like the sweetest compliment. More tears broke free and he cupped my cheek for a moment as though I were something coveted and precious to him. And for a single moment, I think I wanted to be.

Then he walked out of the room, leaving me cold and alone once more. I frowned at the bowl of food he'd brought me. Why did he constantly feed me? Why let me speak to Renzo? Why act like he cared one moment only to threaten me the next? He made no sense.

9

EMILIA

I sat in the middle of my bed, the banging of pots in the kitchen signaling Giovanni's arrival. Apparently, he liked to cook in the evenings. He also got pissed when I didn't eat. Last night he literally stood there in the doorway and watched me eat a bowl of pasta. I'd never admit it, but it might have been the best thing I'd ever tasted. At least if I did have to marry him, I wouldn't have to cook. Silver lining to being forcibly bound to a psychopathic mafia killer. The downside being, oh, everything else.

That wasn't happening, though, because this was it, the moment I'd been planning since I'd gotten off the phone with Renzo yesterday. Escaping was a specialty of mine, and I'd gotten away from my father and his men more times than I could remember. I'd never hurt anyone before, but as I stared down at the small knife in my hand, I realized there was really no other way. I wasn't marrying that man, and going back to Chicago just to be handed off to Matteo wasn't an option. Giovanni wasn't going to let me leave, and as far as I could tell, the key card for the door was on his person at all times. As for the men guarding the place... I'd take his gun and cross that bridge when I got there.

I pushed to my feet and tucked the blade against my wrist, tugging the cuff of Giovanni's shirt down to cover it. My pulse raced as I made my way down the hall. I paused at the end, steeling myself for what I needed to do next.

Giovanni moved around the kitchen with ease, and he almost seemed relaxed. Almost. In the same way a resting lion still twitched its tail. I found myself studying him—the broad muscles of his back, tapered waist, and defined ass. No man had a right to look like that, and the image of his shirtless body was still firmly branded in my mind. He was like some poisonous flower, luring me in with his beauty.

He placed tomatoes on a cutting board and sliced them, his movements careful and concise. *He probably knows his way around a knife, what with all the murdering.* Me, on the other hand...

I pushed the thought away. I had two options—surprise or seduction—because I sure as hell wasn't tackling him head-on. He was a guy and a mafia one at that. Which meant he was stronger, more violent, and far more accomplished in injuring and killing people. I took two steps into the open space before he glanced at me.

"Emilia."

Well, there went surprise. Shit. Could I even seduce him? That one time Matt Jones had kissed me in the girls' locker room did not go any way toward lending me experience here.

"Hey." I tried to keep my voice steady as I awkwardly hopped up onto the kitchen island.

He scraped the tomatoes into the saucepan and turned to face me, thick arms folding over his chest and straining against the material of his shirt. With the prospect of trying to overpower him playing through my mind, he suddenly seemed even bigger, more intimidating.

"What are you making?" Gently, gently. *Lull him into a false sense of security.*

"Bolognese." He stepped toward me. "But that's not why you're really in here, piccola. You don't care what I'm cooking."

"I..." Did he know?

He pressed between my legs, both palms gliding up my thighs and dragging up the material of the shirt. He was careful not to press on the bullet hole he had put in my leg. Even that thought wasn't enough to stop my skin from tingling beneath his warm touch, heart rate ticking up with every inch of ground he made toward my underwear. I could do this. He was making it easy. My hand landed on his chest, trailing up until I gripped the back of his neck.

"You're right. I don't care what you're cooking." When I leaned in and brushed my lips over his jaw, he growled, fingers digging into my hips like he was about to toss me down on the counter and shred the clothing from my body.

This was it. The moment that would define my future. I could barely breathe for fear, but I hoped he would pass it off as arousal. Guilt ate away at me because I wasn't like him. I wasn't a killer, and he'd saved me once, saved my brother...

But he was still my captor, and I would never bow to captivity or to the whims of men like my uncle. His lips teased over my throat, and for a second, everything just stopped. The way he held me, touched me, wanted me... For a second, this felt like something more, like fate, but this was where I killed fate. Pulling the blade free from my sleeve, I gripped the back of his neck tight. And then I drove the knife toward his chest. He jerked back, swatting me away faster than I thought possible and diverting the blow, but not before it sliced across his ribs. A hiss of pain escaped his teeth, and he clamped one hand over his side while the other wrapped around my wrist, squeezing until the blade clattered to the counter.

"Oh, princess. You hesitated."

My heart leaped into a sprint, fear choking me before his blood-slick hand did. Would he kill me? He wrenched me up against him, fingers digging into my throat hard enough to restrict my air. His nose dragged up my cheek before teeth pinched my jaw.

"I love it when you fight," he groaned. "What were you going to do, Emilia? Kill me and run into the hall where my men are waiting?"

"I wasn't trying to kill you, just hurt you—"

"Enough to escape." He pulled back, that glacial gaze meeting mine. He was always scary, but right now, there wasn't an ounce of mercy to be found in his eyes. This was a man who didn't hesitate. If our roles were reversed, I would be bleeding out on the floor right now.

He laughed, the sound cruel and cutting. "Little word of advice, Emilia. If you ever manage to bury a blade in my chest, you had better make sure you kill me because I will hunt you to the ends of the Earth."

I jumped when he touched the tip of the knife to my thigh, dragging it up the inside of my leg. It was a light scratch, not enough to break the skin, but I shivered in response.

"Are you going to punish me?" I whispered, imagining him ramming that knife into my leg and scarring the other thigh.

"Would you like that?" The blade trailed over my panties, and I sucked in a sharp breath right before he pressed against me harder, trapping the flat edge of the knife between us. Fuck, why was that hot?

"For me to spank you and tie you to my bed." He studied me like he was picturing all the ways he could fuck me and kill me. "I think you would. I think you want this." The grip tightened on my throat, fingers sliding over my skin. He could kill me at any moment, but I instinctively knew he wouldn't.

I felt…alive, on the ragged edge with him. Raspy breaths slipped past my lips as he moved the blade to the base of my throat. He yanked me to the edge of the counter and the layers of material between us did little to buffer the thick press of him against my pussy.

"I know you've pictured me spreading these sweet thighs and taking what's mine, Emilia."

"I'm not yours," I managed to gasp.

"Oh, but you are."

Something feral clawed its way to the surface of my consciousness and made me crave this lethal game. The knife inched down between my heaving breasts, where he sliced the button loose. It skittered over the kitchen tile, and he slid the material to the side, skirting my peaked nipple with the very blade I had just cut him with. I was a slave to sensation, my body paralyzed as my brain fought whatever the hell this was.

"And soon, you'll know it just as surely as if I'd branded my name on you." Another roll of his hips and sparks shot through my core.

"Giovanni—"

"But I don't fuck unwilling women."

Was I unwilling? The thought was a jolting one.

"And as eager as your sweet body is—" he tapped my temple — "this isn't. *Yet*."

"I will never be willing."

The smile that pulled at his lips said he knew something I didn't. "Liar. We both know that if I wanted to, I'd take that sweet virginity, right here on this counter, and you'd moan my name like a good girl."

Oh my God. Venomous words fumbled through my mind but wouldn't quite make it onto my lips. I couldn't help but imagine Giovanni's weight pinning me to the cool surface while he choked me and fucked me... "But I don't just want your body. So...I've considered your deal."

My mind stumbled for a minute before I realized what he meant. Hope rose within me. "You're letting Renzo go?"

"No. But I will make you another deal." He released my throat and swept my hair behind my ear. Blood trailed across my cheek, his gaze intent, studying me like I was something he coveted. Had anyone ever looked at me like that?

He brought his lips to my ear, the woodsy scent of him wrapping around me. "Only when you beg me, when that little pussy is dripping for my cock… then I'll marry you." The smile that graced his lips was every bit as devastating as I knew it would be. He was beautiful, and for a moment, I was seduced by the monster.

It took me a second to absorb his filthy words and realize he'd thrown me a lifeline, a get out of jail free card. "I will never beg you to take away my freedom. So, when I don't and you won't marry me, what then?" Would he let me go? The hope was so tentative.

The smirk that curled the edge of his lip was sinister. "Then I'll give you back to your loving family."

My stomach dropped as my hope withered and died. Anger lanced through me, hot and fast, and I shoved against his chest, though it did nothing. "So it's you or the man who wants me dead?" Sergio, Matteo…it was one and the same. "That's just coercion. I'll never *want* to marry a man who bought me just so he could suck my uncle's dick."

His hand shot out, fingers knotting in my hair and wrenching my head back hard enough to send a sting over my scalp. "What did I just say, Emilia?" I glared at him as hot breath washed over my face. "I said I want that pussy dripping."

So I couldn't simply beg for my life. I had to want him.

I loathed him right then, but if he put his hand between my thighs, he'd find what he was looking for. And I was sure he knew it, knew that I was attracted to him, and he'd backed me into a corner I already had the means to get out of. I just had to beg. Just had to do what he wanted. What my uncle wanted. Only this was worse. At least if he forced me, I could still hold onto my pride, my dignity. He wished to strip me of it.

I flicked my eyes over him, allowing every trace of the disgust I felt to bleed into my expression. "That is never going to happen."

His lips twitched, that infuriatingly sexy smirk cutting across his perfect face. "I can't wait to have my ring on your finger and your blood on my cock, piccola." He almost groaned the words before my palm met his cheek.

The clap of skin on skin startled me. I didn't mean to do that, and I readied myself for the return blow. Instead, he just raked his teeth over his bottom lip and grabbed my hand.

"Keep hurting me, princess." He pressed it against his ribs, the dark material of his shirt soaked through. "It makes me so fucking hard."

I tried to pull away my hand, but he wouldn't let me, imprisoning it beneath his own. "You're sick."

"Yes, I am. But just remember, I could chain you to my bed and take what I want from you, Emilia." His forehead fell to mine, slick fingers twining with my own against his side as though we were somehow bound in a blood vow. "And you would love every second. Then you really would be my good little slave."

As if sensing I had reached my limit, he released me and stepped back. I scrambled off the counter before stumbling away from him. Then practically ran to my room, not because

I was scared, but because part of me wanted what he was offering, something so utterly primal that it went beyond reason.

I could have sworn I heard the low rumble of laughter after my door slammed shut.

10

GIO

M y dick was like stone, and my ribs burned as I stared at the corridor where Emilia had just disappeared. I knew she had that knife, knew the second she started playing nice what she was going to do. I'd never been so eager for someone to stab me. She was everything I wanted to taint and tame.

She hesitated. Definitely wanted me.

I dished up a bowl of spaghetti and took it to her room, prepared to go in there and force-feed her if I had to. But I couldn't. If I went in there right now, I'd end up trying to fuck her. *Not before she begs.* The image of Emilia on her knees had the ache in my dick intensifying. I put the bowl on the floor outside her door and strode to my office. My side was still bleeding, my shirt soaked through, but I had more pressing concerns.

I pulled up the camera feed for her room, and she was just standing there, looking shell-shocked. My bloody handprint was stamped on her throat, a crimson streak marring the smooth skin of her face. She'd never been more beautiful, and I'd never wanted to bury my dick in a woman so much. I unfastened my belt and fisted myself. My hand was still covered in blood, but I didn't care. I watched as she sat on the edge of the bed, so innocent yet tainted by violence right then. I stroked myself hard and fast, ready to come in seconds. When I looked down, my dick was painted red and I groaned, imagining that was what it would look like covered in her virginity. I lost it, balls exploding, body jerking as I came over my own hand. Fuck. My chest heaved as I glanced at the mess on my hand. Blood and come; my new favorite combination.

I glanced back to the camera feed just as Emilia opened the door and picked up the bowl of food. Satisfaction poured through me when she took a bite. Good girl.

Picking up my phone, I called Tommy.

"Yeah?"

"I need you to come to the penthouse and stitch me up."

"Who the fuck got you?" Fury tinged his voice, and I knew he was probably picturing some mob member putting a bullet in me.

"Just fucking get here."

There was a beat of silence. "It was the girl, wasn't it?"

I didn't even get a chance to answer before he started laughing.

"Oh, this is great. Wait 'til I tell Jackson."

"Hurry the fuck up and keep your mouth shut." I hung up and pushed to my feet. I needed to at least shower my own come off before he got here.

I was late, thanks to my little run-in with Emilia's knife. The arches of the Brooklyn Bridge loomed behind me, the steady hum of traffic above blending with the music pulsing from inside the nearby nightclub. My nightclub, Vice.

This was my domain, my normal nightly routine before Emilia, where I straddled the legal and illegal parts of my businesses. There was something settling in the familiarity of coming here, a place I usually lingered until the early hours of the morning. Although I couldn't pretend that I didn't find Emilia's company infinitely more interesting.

Vice was one of the glittering jewels in my own personal empire, each one lending to the image that I was a businessman, above reproach. And the further from reproach *I* was, the more it benefitted the Famiglia. The easier it became for councilmen and mayors and various other high-powered individuals to take my dirty money. Plausible deniability opened more doors than violence ever would. Nero had run New York through fear and blood, but I ran it through the very men who had once stood in our way. If I went down, we all did. It was a house of cards with me perched at the top, towering over them all.

Of course, not all my dealings in the club were legal, hence why I was here tonight.

The scent of trash and the briny tinge of the nearby river lingered in the air as I locked my car and cut across the narrow alley to the back door.

Inside, the walls hummed with each rattling vibration of bass as I moved along the narrow hall and ascended the stairs that led to my office. This corridor was private, used only for my less civilized dealings. The room had one glass wall that overlooked the VIP area and the club below. But my attention fell on the three men in the room. Jackson leaned against the back wall, a scowl fixed on his face. Two of the Pérez brothers were on the couch looking bored.

I took a seat at my desk. "Sorry I'm late. I ran into some trouble." And its name was Emilia Donato.

Leonardo Pérez stood and took a seat across from me. He was the oldest of the Pérez brothers. The rest of them were in their teens, but this little fucker…he was maybe twenty-five.

He wore jeans and a hoody pulled up over dark hair. Tattoos crawled up his neck and over his fingers. He looked like any regular gang banger, but he wasn't. He was vicious and smart and had grown big enough to pose a threat to established cartels like the Sinaloa.

"Leonardo Pérez."

He chucked his chin. His younger brother watched us all through narrowed eyes as though waiting to pounce, which was laughable given the size of Jackson compared to the kid. They raised them savage in Colombia, though.

"Giovanni Guerra." He thrust his hands into his hoody pockets and leaned back in the chair as though he had not a care in the world. "I hear you need la cocaína."

Straight to it. Good. "I hear you want to sell some. So, how much?"

He smirked. "How much do you want?"

No one asked how much you wanted. They offered what they had. So I tested him. "Fifty kilos."

"One million US dollars."

I frowned, my gaze flicking over the kid. I'd assume this was pure bullshit if I didn't know his reputation. "You know I'm desperate. You know you could ask twice that…."

He shrugged, his gaze passing over the VIP area beyond the windows with mild interest. "I could. And I know you'd pay it."

"And yet you undercut my supplier. What do you want?" Nothing was free in this world of blood and money.

He took a cigarette from his pocket and placed it to his lips, lighting it. "I want your business, Mr. Guerra."

Jackson shifted beside me. This guy had a reputation, and I knew Jackson didn't want to deal with them. Nero was loyal to Rafe, but it was short-sighted. The Pérez brothers were already established enough to cause powerful people problems. So I either shunned them to appease said people, or I allied with them, knowing that one day, they were sure to *be* the powerful people. Of course, there were no guarantees, but I had a feeling about this one. He reminded me of a more ruthless, young Nero, and that was terrifying. In a few years, with his brothers at his side, they were going to be a problem, one I wanted to be on the right side of. And the simple fact was, depending solely on Chicago had bitten me in the ass. Putting all our eggs in one basket was stupid.

"I can't make you my sole supplier."

He nodded. "Because Rafael D'Cruze is family."

"Something like that." He was Nero's brother-in-law, married to Una's sister. And if there was one person in this world Nero Verdi didn't go against, it was his wife. None of us did. "And you can't bring it into the city direct."

"Fine. Twenty-five kilos a month. Half a mil."

"You get this first order to me without issues, without *unnecessary attention,* and you have a deal." I held my hand out, and he clasped it. "Oh, and watch out for the Irish."

He smirked, and the look that sparked in his eyes spoke of a blood lust to rival Jackson's. "That won't be a problem." He jerked his head at his brother, and the two of them slipped out of the office like hooded wraiths.

Jackson shook his head at me before pouring a drink from the minibar. "This is a bad idea, Gio. They are absolutely going to draw the kind of attention we don't need right now."

"What we need is product. We're out millions while the fucking Irish are rolling around in coke and money. Our coke, Jackson, our fucking money."

He fell into the chair across from me and tipped his drink back. "I told you, we can handle them."

"And draw the exact attention you're preaching to me about right now." I shook my head. "Tommy bought off the cops in Chicago, so be ready for the call when Hector has the mob's coke seized." I opened my laptop. "You're going to steal it back."

He snorted. "You want me to steal from the police, the coke that they seized from the mob, that they stole from us."

"Exactly."

He lifted a brow. "It's actually brilliant."

"Not just a pretty face."

"Don't know what you're on about. You're an ugly fuck." He downed the remainder of his drink before pushing to his feet. "I'll handle it, and Gio?"

I glanced up at him. "Yeah?"

"Don't go getting your throat slit by the girl in your bed."

"Fucking Tommy."

His laughter rose over the music as he walked down the stairs. I might even risk getting my throat cut to have Emilia Donato in my bed.

I stayed at the club for a few hours, catching up on paperwork. It was gone midnight when my phone rang, Philipe's name flashing over the screen. He was on Emilia-babysitting duty.

"What?" I snapped.

"The girl escaped."

I swear I felt the vein in my temple throb and my teeth ground together. "What?"

"We got her back, but she started a fire and knocked out Nick." How the hell did that tiny girl knock out a guy Nick's size? *The same way she cut me?* The thought was like a grenade with the pin pulled. If she touched another man, there would be no amount of begging that could save her from me. And if Nick touched her… he was a dead man.

I got up and grabbed my jacket. "I'm on my way. Don't leave her unattended until I get there." Of all the spoiled brats in the world…

By the time I made it home, it was after one in the morning, and my rage was palpable, tinging my vision red. Philipe was standing outside the door to my apartment, his face serious and shoulders tense.

"She's inside."

"Where's Nick?"

"Sent him home. She broke his nose."

I let out a hard breath, willing a sense of calm that was very much absent. "Explain."

"The fire alarm was going off. When Nick saw smoke coming under the door, he rushed in, and she nailed him in the face with a bar stool."

Of course, she did. My shoulders relaxed slightly at the knowledge that she didn't get close to him.

"She stole his gun, too, but I guess she doesn't know how to use one." She could have shot herself, for fuck's sake.

"You can go."

He left, and I opened the door to the apartment. The smell of smoke hit me straight away. The oven door was open, foam and water dripping onto the flooded wooden floor. Everything around the oven was black from the smoke and soot, and I knew it would all have to be replaced. My temper spiked, creeping into territory she really did not want to witness. When I walked into her room, Emilia was sitting on the edge of the bed waiting for me. Her gaze met mine, teeth digging into her bottom lip nervously. At least she had the sense to fear me.

"Tell me, Emilia, do you wish to die?"

Because she might well if she went out there alone. Sergio had made it clear that he had no qualms about putting a bullet in her head.

She pushed to her feet, squaring her shoulders for a fight. "Are you threatening me?"

Damn. That fire made me want to spank her ass until she learned exactly when to bite her damn tongue.

"Because I'm not just going to accept being your captive and obey you like some pet."

The thin, ragged string of my patience snapped, and the side of myself that I kept leashed slipped a little. Grabbing her by the throat, I slammed her up against the screened wall, making the TV flicker. Those rose-pink lips parted on a ragged gasp, and her pulse raced beneath my fingertips like a hummingbird's wings.

"Oh, but right now, that's exactly what you are, sweetheart. A pet that is safe because for now, I want you that way." My thigh pushed between hers and the full weight of my body crushed her tiny form. "Or would you rather we call off our arrangement and you go back to your family?" I smiled when she tensed. "Ah, there it is. That fear that tells me you aren't completely reckless." Not fear of me, though.

She was scared of Sergio Donato more than me, and if she were anyone else, that would be a grave error in judgment.

"Fuck you." She rammed her palm into my chest and dug her nails into the base of my throat. *Yes, fight me, sweet Emilia.* "I won't apologize for wanting to be free of you *and* them."

"You set fire to my fucking apartment. Again."

She stared me down with nothing but hatred and unbending will, and my dick pressed against the front of my pants. I didn't give a shit if she felt it either. Leaning in, I nipped her ear lobe, riding the fine line of my control as her breath hitched in response.

"Careful, piccola. Anyone would think you like my rage."

She lifted her chin defiantly.

"Or maybe it's just those daddy issues."

Her palm met my cheek in a resounding clap that sent all the blood in my body to my dick. When was the last time a woman was brave enough to strike me? Never. It was always submission and eagerness to please. Yet, that was the third time she'd struck me in less than a week. I was growing addicted to her temper.

My hand shifted, and I lifted her onto tiptoes, cutting off her air as I brought her lips to mine. Just a brush but enough to have me biting back a groan. "I could kill you and save myself a lot of hassle."

"But you won't," she choked out.

"You think I need you?"

"No." Her lips caressed mine as she spoke, and fuck, I wanted to kiss her, just to see if she tasted of innocence and sunshine. "I think you want me."

I stroked her hair away from her face. "And you think that'll save you?"

"You won't hurt me," she breathed.

I traced her bottom lip, and a trembling breath washed over my fingertip in response. "So innocent. So naïve." The urge to dominate her was like a devil on my shoulder. "So fucking hopeful."

"What are you going to do?" She had no idea that those whispered words of trepidation only fed the beast that sought to destroy her.

"I'm going to punish you, princess." I shouldn't have liked anything about this, but my heart thumped hard in anticipation, my dick throbbing painfully.

"You don't scare me, Giovanni." And there was the fire, the sour cutting through the sweet in such a heady combination. She couldn't hide the tremor in her voice, though. Brave, foolish, and so perfect.

"And *that* is your mistake."

11

EMILIA

Giovanni Guerra was like a priceless oil painting made up of perfect strokes, but if you scratched that first layer of paint away, beneath would be another image—one of blood and shadows. That was what I saw now, what I had seen the night he'd found me. This side of him was as terrifying as it was intriguing. This was the man my family feared, a beast I wanted to both run from and tame. And every inch of him pressed against me, his fingers cutting off my air, hot breath washing over my lips like sweet poison, begging me to taste it.

His gaze dropped to my mouth, and the grip on my throat loosened just enough to allow me a gasp of uninhibited air. The space between us crackled with a dangerous kind of tension, one that would combust if I weren't careful. But some sick, twisted part of me wanted him to squeeze a little harder, to lean in and kiss me with the same lips that would threaten to kill me. That feral flicker took root in his eyes, his jaw clenching before he snatched my wrist and dragged me to the bed. I nearly choked on my own heartbeat when he shoved me down onto the mattress.

There was a clink as something tightened around my wrist, and when I tried to move, I couldn't. I glanced at the leather cuff now restraining me to the bed, wondering where the hell it had come from. He'd tied me to the bed.

"What the fuck are you doing?"

I kicked out at him, snarling and raking the nails of my free hand over his cheek before he slammed my other arm against the headboard with a crack of pain. He cuffed that one, too. A chain clinked when I fought against it, my heart pounding in my chest like a trapped bird throwing itself against a window. I recoiled into the headboard as he loomed over me. This was it. He was finally done waiting or asking…

"Giovanni, don't. Please…"

Instead of coming closer, he stepped back, chest heaving, fists clenching at his sides. Without another word, he turned and strode out of the bedroom. My moment of relief was short-lived before I was spitting mad again. Who the hell had cuffs just attached to their spare bed, hidden and waiting to be used? Of course, that was a rabbit hole my inexperienced brain really didn't need to travel down. And yet, I imagined him coming back in here, touching me, kissing me, teasing me while I was restrained and at his mercy. Heat unfurled within me like a cat stretching from a long slumber. I didn't want that, did I? A fantasy, non-psycho version of him, maybe…

"You bastard! Come back here and let me go."

Nothing. Silence. The shackles were tight enough to allow very little movement, but there was some… enough.

It took me twenty minutes to work my right hand out of that leather cuff before I could free myself. The skin around my wrists was chaffed and red from my efforts. It wasn't the only thing that was red. My vision was tinged crimson as I stormed down the hall to his room.

When I shoved open the door, it was dark inside except for a shaft of light spilling from the bathroom. Giovanni stood in the closet doorway in just a towel. His hair was wet, drops of water glistening in the light as they rolled down the tanned skin of his chest like little diamonds. A few cut through the valley of his abs in a way that made me lose my train of thought. Holy shit.

"Emilia." His voice was a low growl. A warning if ever I heard one.

"You can't just tie me to a bed!" I snapped, my anger returning as soon as I tore my attention from that body. I went to step into his room, but he held up a finger.

"Walk into this room and you had better be prepared for the consequences."

That was when I took in the rigid set of his body, his hands clamped on the closet door frame, jaw ticcing erratically. A flicker of awareness took root; the rational voice in the back of my mind told me to turn around and run. That I wasn't ready for whatever was about to happen next. But the other part of me rose up, taking the challenge, refusing to back down.

"What are you going to do? Hurt me?" Then I brazenly stepped over the threshold like I was so smart, proving a point.

He stormed the distance between us, something completely rabid flashing in his eyes before he grabbed my jaw hard enough to bruise. He shattered every expectation I had when his lips slammed over mine. I froze, but he wouldn't allow my lack of participation. His lips were demanding, totally unforgiving, taking from me everything I didn't even know I wanted to give him until that moment. I'd never really been kissed properly before, and I didn't know what I thought it would be like—sweet, chaste, careful? But Giovanni kissed me like I owed him something and he was there to collect. It was lips and tongue and teeth. Angry, lashing strokes that punished until I tasted the metallic tang of my own blood. My fingers went to his hair, his hands bruising my thighs as he lifted and pinned me to the wall. It was like my body wasn't even my own in that moment. I was lost to him. Wanted him. *Needed* him.

And then he was gone. I stumbled on my feet as he forced distance between us, his chest heaving as he watched me try to catch my breath. Every inch of skin was tingling and sparking where he'd touched me.

"Leave, Emilia." When I didn't immediately do so, his hand slammed into the wall beside my head. "Now!"

I jumped and numbly staggered into the hall, confused by what the hell had just happened. When I climbed into bed, I could still feel his kiss branding my lips. A kiss I should have hated, one I definitely didn't. Then again, maybe I would have liked any kiss. It was my first real one. Compared to that, Matt Jones pecking me on the lips did not count.

I swiped my tongue over my bottom lip and winced at the sting from the small wound there.

It took what felt like forever to calm my racing heart enough for sleep to find me, and when it did, my dreams weren't full of the murderous, dark creatures from previous nights; they were filled with sapphire eyes and harsh touches that I craved.

———

When I ventured out of my room the next day, the entire apartment still smelled like smoke, and the kitchen was pretty badly damaged. At the time, it seemed ingenious, putting a pan of oil in the oven. There I was, thinking it would smoke and set off the alarm, and it worked, right up until it burst into uncontrollable flames. Guilt niggled at me for launching the barstool at that guy, but it wasn't like I could get past him fairly. Not that it mattered. Four men were waiting for me the second the elevator doors opened in the lobby. Just like Giovanni had said they would be. I was reckless, but not "take on guys with guns" reckless.

In the cold light of day, shame had set in over what had happened last night. I had kissed Giovanni, and I was mortified. So to avoid bumping into him—not the easiest feat in his own damn apartment—I took a cup of coffee up to the roof. I half expected the door to be locked again or for him to have fitted extra security, but he hadn't. Yet.

I spent most of the afternoon sitting up there, a blanket pulled around me to fight off the first chill of fall in the air. For a moment, I tried to picture what my life would be like if I lived here, if I married him.

How long did I have until I had to make a decision? How long to try to escape again? Freedom had never felt so far away, and I was going to be forced to choose between the devil and the deep blue sea. It felt like I had a noose around my neck, and my toes were barely clinging to the edge of the stool I was standing on.

The sun was high in the sky when the door to the roof swung open. I expected Giovanni, but instead, Tommy appeared. His red hair caught in the bright light as he flashed me a wide smile. He was wearing a suit and had a plastic bag in one hand.

"Hey. What are you doing here?" I unfolded my legs, ready to get away from him. Was this it? Had Giovanni finally had enough and sent him to take me back to Chicago?

"Calm down. Gio asked me to come. Let me in himself."

I frowned at that for multiple reasons. The main one being that Gio was actually here. I'd seen no trace of him.

"Like what you've done with the place, by the way. The odor d'bonfire really brings that rustic vibe." A smirk cut over his lips. "Not sure Gio's thrilled."

I rolled my eyes, fighting a smile. "He's still mad then?" Mad might have been an understatement. The man had tied me to a bed.

"He's an uptight bastard, but he'll forget all about it soon." I wasn't sure either of us was forgetting last night anytime soon. My wounded lip throbbed at the memory. "He's gone out, anyway."

"And you're here to babysit." I hadn't thought about the fact that if I failed in my attempt, then my security would get even tighter. Dammit. I could feel that noose tightening.

"Just stopping you burning yourself alive, that's all." He took a seat on the couch beside me, then placed the plastic bag down between us. "That's for you."

I frowned as I took it, peering inside at the sketchbook and pack of art pencils. It was just paper and pencils, but for some reason, a wave of emotion rose, a lump forming in my throat.

"You bought this? For me?"

"Gio asked me to get it." That was…nice of him.

"Thank you." I told myself I was grateful to Tommy for getting the stuff. Not to Giovanni for noticing anything about me or making the request. It was hard not to be a little bit grateful, though.

"Just try not to shank me with a pencil." He smirked, leaning back on the couch.

"I probably should." I laughed. "You know, escape before he hands me back to my family." I was half-joking, but I sure as hell was not begging him to marry me, so… half not.

The smile fell from Tommy's face. "Would marrying Gio really be so bad? He's not a horrible guy, you know. He used to be the moral one."

A horn blared in the distance, cutting through the slice of peace up here. "What happened?"

"Life. Reality. No one can sit on the throne without being willing to spill a lot of blood," he murmured, and I hated that the easy smile was now nowhere to be seen. I felt like I'd stolen his joy. "Your family is no different, Emilia."

"I know." I didn't know first hand, but I knew what they did.

"But Gio would never hurt one of his own. He's loyal."

I turned away from him, glancing over Giovanni's city, his empire. "Why are you saying this?"

"I think you could be good for him." I met his gaze once more. "And I think your family is despicable for trying to kill you."

It wasn't them, though. It was Matteo. The very man I'd end up with. I'd been trying to ignore that fact, telling myself I would escape, but what if I couldn't? I didn't want to talk about this.

"How is Renzo?" I asked because I knew Tommy had been with him. I held my breath, fully expecting him not to tell me anything.

"Good. He's up and moving. Our doc did a pretty good job of putting him back together."

I released the breath, my shoulders relaxing with it. "What's going to happen to him, Tommy?"

He shrugged. "I don't know. I don't make those kinds of decisions, and I don't want to give you false hope."

My heart plummeted in my chest, and his hand gripped my arm.

"But I will say that Gio doesn't harm anyone unless it serves a purpose, and I can't see what purpose that would serve."

I could. He knew Renzo was my weak spot. Giovanni had

made it very clear he wanted me to marry him with the premise of willingness. He hadn't directly threatened Renzo, but I'd come to expect the worst because anything less was just stupid.

———

A couple of hours later and I came to the annoying realization that I liked Tommy. He was charming and funny and made me smile far too easily. But I didn't want to like the guy who had once put a gun to my brother's head, no matter if it was "just business." I didn't want to like anyone or anything attached to Giovanni's life.

He checked his watch and pushed to his feet. "Come on. I'm hungry."

"I think there's food—"

"Please, Gio doesn't have junk food."

"Okay…."

"His version of dirty food is pasta and only because it's his nostalgic guilty pleasure." He started toward the door. "Tell me you don't just want a bag of chips or a soda."

Now that he mentioned it, I did. Even the take-out that I'd refused to eat was kind of healthy. Salads, subs, sushi. Giovanni didn't get those perfect abs on just pasta, that was for sure. "Maybe."

"Come on then."

I followed him down the stairs, fully expecting him to order from somewhere. When he headed for the front door, I paused. "Wait. You're taking me outside?" A bolt of excitement shot through me, but I glanced down at Gio's dress shirt I was wearing. "Like this?"

He paused for a second before unfastening his belt.

I held my hand up, shielding my view. "Um, if you're going to drop your pants, please warn me."

He laughed before passing his belt around my waist and tightening it. "There. You look great." He winked at me. "We'll be ten minutes. He'll never even know."

Somehow, I thought he would, but I wasn't turning down the chance to escape.

12

GIO

I washed the blood from my hands and forearms, unable to do anything about the obvious splits and bruising across my knuckles. I slipped on a clean shirt before leaving my room and descending the stairs into the main body of the house. Screams echoed along the corridor, drifting up from the basement where I'd left our latest mob captive with Jackson. At least our little war was keeping my enforcer happy. Jackson was ruthless at the best of times, but with a rat in our close ranks, he was exceptionally driven. And that guy was the lone survivor from a group who'd tried to steal a shipment we had just taken from the Chicago PD. How the hell did they know what we were doing?

Another scream rang through the house before it cut off, and I wondered if the man was dead or just unconscious. No, he'd be unconscious. Jackson would keep injecting him with adrenaline, bringing him back from the edge over and over until the guy broke. Though I'd just taken out every inch of my recent frustrations on him and he hadn't said a word.

I grabbed my phone and car keys from the kitchen counter, frowning when I read over a text from Philipe.

"Tommy took Emilia out of the apartment."

Why the fuck would he do that? She'd one hundred percent take the opportunity to run. Dammit. I left and got into my car, calling Tommy as I floored it down the drive. Of course, he didn't pick up. The thought of anything happening to her had a horrible sense of fear skittering over my skin, the likes of which I hadn't felt in a long time. Shit. Did I care about her, or was I just obsessed with her?

When I made it back to the city and walked into my apartment, Tommy and Emilia were sitting on the couch laughing, a bag of chips between them. In an instant, Tommy's smiling fucking face became the focus of all my rage.

"What the fuck, Tommy?"

"We went to get supplies." He shrugged. *Shrugged.*

I glanced at Emilia, unable to stop my gaze from roaming over her, looking for injury. The only one I found was the little purple bruise on her bottom lip from that kiss last night. If I could even call it that. It was more like a damn attack. However, my attention quickly shifted to her exposed legs, my shirt barely reaching past her ass, a belt cinching her small waist. He took her outside dressed like that. I was going to kill him. Slowly. Painfully.

"You took her outside where she might escape, or where The Outfit might get her, for fucking snacks."

Emilia flinched at my raised voice.

Tommy just folded his arms over his chest. "Fine. No popsicle for you."

My eye was twitching. "Tommy!"

"What do you mean, The Outfit might get me?" Emilia asked, her voice barely above a whisper.

"They tried to kill you once. You don't have the protection of my name. Out there, you're fair game."

The color seemed to drain from her cheeks. Good. I needed her to know what was at stake here. I didn't mention the fact that Sergio would actually probably just marry her off elsewhere. I didn't need her thinking she had any other option but me.

Tommy huffed out a sigh. "Don't pretend your guys weren't following us. If she'd escaped, they would have caught her, but she wasn't going to, were you Emilia?"

She shook her head like some scared little lamb. I hated it. Hated that two minutes ago, she'd been laughing with someone who wasn't me. Hated that I gave a single shit about her happiness beyond making her scream my name.

"And even The Outfit aren't stupid enough to kill her in broad daylight in the middle of New York."

It was highly unlikely, but I didn't care. It was as though one kiss had exacerbated my obsession tenfold. I had to go out tonight. Tommy was supposed to watch Emilia, but I couldn't handle the thought of having her away from me where I couldn't see her. Fuck, I was losing it. "I'm taking her with me tonight."

She would certainly make a boring affair much more interesting. All part of my legitimate image. Successful businessman, charitable donor, and all-around saint. Torture at five and raising money for orphans at eight.

"Call Naomi and get her a dress."

He cocked a brow. "You're taking her to a gala? You just said she was a flight risk."

"Not with me, she isn't." I glanced at Emilia, and she shifted in her seat as though my attention made her uncomfortable.

The slight blush that tinged her cheeks said it had nothing to do with fear. My gaze dropped to her bare legs, skimming over the bandage that covered her thigh. People out there had seen all that golden skin, and an irrational surge of anger tore through me at the thought.

"And get her some other clothes while you're there."

"I'm not a personal shopper, for fuck's sake."

"Well, you are now. " I snapped at him, still pissed. "Go."

He shook his head as he got up and walked away, his phone already pressed to his ear.

Emilia pushed to her feet, a frown pulling her brows together. "You mean to tell me I've been here for a week, and I could have had clothes this whole time, but instead, I had to steal shirts from your closet because you wouldn't even give me that?"

I couldn't fight the smile that tugged at my lips. "I like you in my clothes." My dick liked it, too, which was reason enough why I should have given her clothes of her own long before now. "Be ready at seven."

I expected her to argue, but she didn't, and that was always cause for suspicion. Oh, my little kitten was considering how she would escape me out in public. This time I managed to hold my smile as I closed the gap between us. She tilted back her chin, her gaze holding mine with a bravery that made me want to test it. I glanced at her bruised bottom lip and couldn't find it in me to feel guilty. I liked that I'd marked her, that the evidence of my lips was imprinted on hers. Taking her jaw, I pulled her up onto her tiptoes until her hand landed against my chest for balance.

"Please run tonight, piccola. I'll enjoy chasing and punishing you again."

She offered me a smile that bordered on a snarl. "The next time you tie me to a bed and leave me there, I'll do a damn sight worse than come into your room."

"Promises, promises, princess." I pictured her tying me to a bed, crawling over me, and putting her lips on my body. Submission wasn't my thing, but for her, it might just be. "But just know, next time, I won't be walking away and letting you off so easily. That was an intro."

Her lips curled in a small smile that went right to my dick. "Promises, promises." Oh, she was playing with fire, and we were both going to burn.

"Begging and dripping, piccola."

The blush that stained her cheeks had me biting back a groan. I slammed my mouth over hers without thought. The taste of her rolled over me like expensive whiskey burning through my veins. When I forced myself to pull away, Emilia gaped at me, lips swollen, cheeks pink, eyes wild. She was the most beautiful creature I'd ever seen, and I wanted nothing more than to bend her over that couch and fuck my name from her lips. But she hadn't begged…

Before she could speak, I turned away. "Be ready at seven, Emilia."

I checked my reflection, adjusting the bowtie before I stepped out of my room and knocked on Emilia's door. When she opened it, I was ready to murder Tommy for the second time today. I couldn't take her out in public like that. The red dress clung to every damn curve, a split exposing the entire length of her uninjured leg, neckline plunging between her perky tits.

"Is that the only dress Tommy gave you?"

Her brows pulled together before she folded her arms over her chest, covering the strip of skin between her breasts. "Yes, and for your information, this wouldn't be my first choice, either." Her gaze dropped to the floor. "But seeing as I look so awful, maybe you should just leave me here."

"I'm not leaving you here because I don't trust you out of my sight, piccola."

She took a step back, and I chased her, the same way I always seemed to.

"And you don't look awful; you look fucking edible. Which is a problem because I can't spill blood in civil company."

Even through her makeup, I could see her cheeks tinge pink. "Whatever. This is stupid."

I loved how awkwardly she reacted to any kind of compliment.

I pulled a box from my pocket and popped it open.

Her eyes widened when she took in the enormous ruby inside. "What the hell is that?" She pointed at it like it might jump out and bite her.

"That is the ring I would have given you the day you ran away from the engagement party." A family heirloom of sorts, the only thing I had left of my mother. I remembered pulling up to that party and hating that I was about to put something so valuable to me on the finger of a girl I didn't even know. I'd only known Emilia for a week, but I knew this ring would never sit on anyone else's finger as perfectly as it would hers.

She was rigid as I slid it into place, the rock almost the width of her slim finger. Some deep-seated part of me practically purred at the sight of it, as though I'd tattooed my name on her damn forehead. That ring marked her as mine, and no one would fuck with what belonged to me. Not even The Outfit if they knew what was good for them.

"I'm not marrying you." Emilia's wide-eyed gaze met mine. "I didn't beg you," she whispered.

"No, but you will." I threaded my fingers through her hair and pressed my lips into the mass of messy curls. "For the sake of appearances, though, you are mine. We are engaged, and that is how you will be introduced."

"Won't that seem a bit weird? I mean, why don't you just say I'm your date or your girlfriend?"

"Because I don't date and I don't have girlfriends." I gripped her hand and pulled her down the hallway, her high heels clicking over the hardwood. "There are girls I fuck, and now there is the girl I'll marry."

She fell into silence, and I hoped that maybe, just maybe, she was finally understanding. She would be mine, and trying to run from that was pointless.

13

EMILIA

Giovanni pulled to a stop outside the opera house, where a crowd gathered on either side of a short red carpet. When he said gala, I didn't picture quite such a spectacle, and my stomach clenched with nerves.

"Did you really bring me here just to keep an eye on me? Or did you just want to parade me around with this rock on my finger like some prize?"

His gaze swept over me, bruised knuckles brushing over my cheek so gently it was almost reverent. "I know you're going to try to run. You will undoubtedly fail, but on the off chance you succeed, I want Sergio Donato to have no question of who you belong to and who will be coming for him should any harm befall you."

"I…" My heart skittered, something warm and comforting settling in my chest.

Was this…what it felt like to be cared for in some way? No, he didn't care. He was possessive of his things, that was all.

"Make no mistake, I would be forced to kill him, and that would be detrimental right now." His thumb dragged over my bottom lip, over the bruise he'd put there. "So if you can't behave, then you will at least smile and make the entire world believe you are mine as assuredly as I do."

This right here was my perfect opportunity to escape, so if I had to play a part until then, I would.

"I've been lenient with you, piccola, but don't test me tonight." Giovanni Guerra was many things, but lenient was not one of them.

Beneath that immaculate tux and the gleaming smile was a savage. He got out of the car and opened my door. I took his offered hand, and he pulled me to my feet before brushing his lips over my fingers, over the ring that sat there like a tiny shackle.

We walked toward the building, the ruby like a ten-ton weight, a flashing neon light signaling my status—sold, bought, owned. Cameras flashed as we approached the front door, and I painted a smile on my face. Not like I wasn't used to this. I'd spent my whole life in the upper echelons of Chicago's corrupt society, pretending to be the perfect daughter of a violent man, paraded for a day when one of his fellow awful associates would want to marry me.

This was different, though. This was public. The real, law-abiding public. The reporters barked rapid-fire questions at us. *Who am I? Are we engaged? How long have we been together? When is the wedding?* I glanced at Giovanni for cues, but his face was set in that stoney mask. Totally unreadable. He acted as though he didn't even hear them, like they were beneath him, irrelevant.

The skirt of my dress swished around my legs as he led me inside. The chaos seemed to die down for a moment as we moved into a lobby with a grand staircase sweeping up both sides of the space. The moment we stepped through a set of double doors, the tinkling of glasses and the low hum of chatter bombarded me. The ballroom was made up of glittering chandeliers and tables dressed with flowers. Waiters circulated trays of champagne flutes among a crowd of people in expensive dresses and suits. It was so familiar, yet not. This was not a room full of sharks. These people were small fish, and Giovanni was a great white cruising among them. Attention shifted to us, people subtly moving away because even if they couldn't pinpoint it, they sensed the predator among them.

It didn't stop more than one woman eyeing him like their next meal, though, right before their glares settled on me. Giovanni was beautiful and powerful; of course, they wanted him. I hated everything he represented, but on a purely lust-based level, *I* wanted him. And didn't that make me worse than them all? I knew the creature that lurked beneath that pretty face. He'd taken my brother, held me captive, was still trying to manipulate me into a so-called willing marriage, and yet I couldn't deny that I liked his touch, craved his attention. I always thought I was relatively untouched by the corruption that ruled my father's world, but I had to ask myself if that was true because something had to be fundamentally wrong with me.

Giovanni led me to a round table full of people and pulled out my chair like the perfect gentleman. When I was seated, he snagged a glass of champagne from a waiter and placed it in front of me before sitting. He was the picture of perfect refinement as he introduced me to these strangers as his fiancée. Politicians, musicians, bankers… people of influence and wealth, and all of them knew him.

For the first time, I realized Giovani Guerra was not like my father or my uncle. He wasn't hiding in the shadows, running his dark underworld with threats and fear. No, he was rubbing shoulders with the very men who would condemn him if they knew what he was. Or maybe they did know, maybe he was lining their pockets, too, and greed simply outweighed morals. Wasn't that the way of the world?

I saw the interest in their eyes as they looked at me, the judgment. Why was Giovanni Guerra marrying some nineteen-year-old girl no one had ever seen before? Why indeed. I chugged the glass of champagne before swiping another from a passing tray. I was going to have to get drunk to get through this.

I stilled when Giovanni swept my hair from my neck, his hot breath trickling over my skin as he leaned in. "Don't drink too much." He disguised his warning with the soft brush of his lips beneath my ear, and I sucked in a sharp breath.

When he resettled in his seat, I held his gaze before lifting the new glass to my lips and downing the whole thing. He could go fuck himself. He cocked a brow before lifting his right hand and tapping one finger over his left bicep. I wrote it off as a tick or something until fifteen minutes later when some politician's wife asked me when the wedding was.

The alcohol had already gone to my head slightly and defiance was still burning through my veins like acid. "Oh, I'm not actually marrying him. I'm just in it for the big rock. He's here for my body."

Her face blanched, though she tried to cover it with a polite smile. When I glanced at Giovanni, he tapped two fingers over his arm this time, and now it was very clearly more than a tick.

"Is that supposed to mean something to me?"

One finger slid along my jaw before stopping beneath my chin and hooking me closer. "Strike two." There was a sensual edge to his voice that trickled over my skin along with a shiver of warning. A sense of danger danced in the air between us, daring me.

"How many strikes do I get?" My voice was barely above a whisper.

His gaze dropped to my lips. "Three."

"And what happens when I get to three?"

"Then I punish your bratty ass, Emilia." Why did that sound so tempting? "But keep pushing. I'll enjoy it far more than you will, I promise you."

That feral spark ignited in his eyes, and it sucked me in, making me want to dance with the beast that lingered beneath that veil of civility. Heat crept through me in a slow, rolling fog that blinded me to everything but him, the sharp cut of his cheekbones, those eyes that could be both ice cold and red hot in the same breath. When the tension wound tight enough to snap, I pulled away. I needed to clear my head and remember why the hell I was here. It wasn't to play sexy little games with my captor.

"I, uh, I need to go to the bathroom," I stammered.

His lips twitched as he adjusted his bowtie, the piece of satin so out of place against the tattoos that crawled over his collar. "Behave, piccola."

I pushed to my feet and stumbled away, drunk, partly on champagne, and partly from his presence. I had to get a grip and remember how much I hated him. This was my chance. The first time I'd been out of that apartment since he'd caught me. I wanted to rip this damn ring off my finger and drop it into a passing champagne glass, but I could pawn it, and I'd undoubtedly need the money if I was going to outrun Giovanni and my uncle. I knew the risk, knew that my family might hunt me down, but I couldn't settle for living in a cage just to stay safe.

Skirting down a hallway, I glanced over my shoulder, fully expecting him to be following me. And if not him, then some of his henchmen, but I saw no one other than stuffy-looking gala attendees. Surely he didn't actually trust me? The whole reason he'd brought me here was to watch me, yet here I was, strolling around on my own. Once in the bathroom, I pretended to fix my makeup while waiting for the two women in there to leave. Then I locked the door and walked over to the sole window, which was narrow and high up.

Grabbing the wastepaper bin, I turned it over and climbed up, shoving the glass open as far as it would go. Beyond the window was a dark alley that ran down the side of the opera house. My heart pounded out a staccato beat as I waited for the door to explode open, for Giovanni to trap me like the devil he was and drag me back to hell. But he didn't. The only sound was the low hum of music from the ballroom. I pulled myself up on the narrow ledge and debated taking off my shoes, but I'd rather break an ankle than go barefoot in a New York alley.

I squeezed through the gap, the material of my dress snagging on a catch with a defined rip as I lay down and slid sideways through the narrow opening. Breath hissed through my teeth as my wounded leg pressed against the wooden frame, my hips barely fitting through. I'd always been jealous of Chiara's butt, but right now, I was grateful for my lack of an ass. I could only imagine the humiliation of Giovanni finding me wedged in a window.

The dim glow of a streetlight cast shadows over a dumpster right below the window. I clung to the ledge, breaking a nail and scraping my hands before I landed on top of it, then scrambled to the ground, all without breaking my ankle. Elation washed through me, the garbage-tainted air suddenly seeming so fresh, so free. Now all I had to do was get the hell out of New York before Giovanni found me.

14

EMILIA

My tentative optimism was short-lived. The second I took a step toward the mouth of the alley, a figure separated from the darkness, stepping into my path. His arms were folded over his chest, the low light playing through red hair. Tommy. Letting out a sigh, I tried to hide the crushing sense of defeat. I should have known Giovanni would never just let me go to the bathroom on my own.

"You just lost me a hundred bucks, kid."

"You bet I wouldn't try and escape?"

He shrugged. "Thought you knew better than to think he wouldn't be prepared."

I frowned. "You know, you could just let me go. I can… I can pay you—"

"No, you can't."

My temper reared its head. "And if I could? Would that make you less inclined to hand me over to be married and bedded against my will?"

His brows crumpled as he took a step toward me. "Gio isn't a bad guy, Emilia. He's certainly not going to rape you—"

"Just marry me and take my freedom?" Funny how one seemed abhorrent to him but the other didn't. Truthfully, I'd rather give my body than my freedom.

He let out a sigh and looked past me as though he could direct his frustration at the brick walls surrounding us. "I saw one of your father's capos put a gun to your head, Emilia." His gaze snapped back to mine, the green of his irises bright in the darkness. "You think if you escape, that will be it? That you'll skip off into the sunset? Gio is the lesser of all your evils here."

The unfairness of it all suddenly felt like a lead weight crushing me. "I didn't ask for any of this."

He stepped forward, and before I could object, he pulled me into a hug. I went limp in his arms as tears threatened.

"I'm sorry. It's not right, but I promise you, he won't hurt you. He protects those who are loyal to him."

I wasn't, though, and I never truly would be. They both had to know that.

"Come on." He pulled away and slung an arm around my shoulders, leading me down the alley. "He'll be wondering where you are."

"You were waiting for me, Tommy. I'd say he knows exactly where I am."

"Well, he can't say you aren't a fighter, sweetheart."

He walked me around the front of the building and back inside the glittering ballroom as though he'd just happened upon me.

Day by day, move by failed move, I was losing hope. I might never escape, and then I'd be forced to make a choice that wasn't really a choice.

Giovanni's expression gave nothing away as Tommy pulled out my chair.

"Thank you, Tommy," I said through gritted teeth as I smoothed my dress beneath my thighs.

And then he left. I wanted to hate Tommy every bit as much as I hated his boss, but it was impossible. There was something about him that spoke of kindness in a world where I'd rarely experienced it, and I wished he could stay instead of leaving me to the wolves, or rather, wolf. If anyone else at the table wondered why I was being escorted back from the bathroom, they didn't say anything.

I refused to look at Giovanni, focusing on the plate of food that had been served in my absence. Lamb shank and vegetables. A fancy version, of course. Fingers brushed my chin, and Giovanni forced my gaze to his, thumb swiping the corner of my lip.

"Third strike." A wicked smirk played over his lips. "And I thought this evening would be disappointing." His words were ice, eyes promising retribution.

With that, he released me and turned away, starting a conversation with the banker on his other side. I sat there, a knot in my stomach, shoulders tense, waiting for the ax to fall. Because there was no way he'd just let it go. Would he hurt me? As the minutes ticked by, I stupidly started to relax, picking at my food and draining another glass of wine. Giovanni laughed at some joke I hadn't paid attention to, his hand landing on my thigh almost casually. Of course, nothing he did was casual. Warm fingers slid into the split of my dress, traveling up and dragging both the skirt and table cloth to my hips. My pulse ticked up, blood roaring in my ears as my body trembled. With fear? Anticipation? I really wasn't sure. When he brushed my underwear, my hand shot out, gripping his wrist.

"Tsk tsk, piccola." His lips pressed to my temple, and to anyone looking on, he seemed like a sweet and loving fiancé. "You're racking up quite the rap sheet tonight."

I met his gaze, lips so close I could taste the whiskey on his breath. "Please." It was all I could say, though I had no idea if I was begging for—his mercy or his wrath.

He cocked a brow, waiting, and I knew I was making it worse for myself. I released his wrist, and he kissed my forehead, lips lingering on my skin as he slipped one finger past my panties and brushed over my clit. I sucked in a sharp breath, and he picked up his drink, sipping it with the casual grace of a man in absolute control of everything around him. He resumed his conversation with the banker while I couldn't focus on a single thing but him and his fingers. I tried to breathe, to remain calm, but no man had ever touched me like this.

Liquid pleasure trickled through my body, and it took everything in me to remain still while he stroked lazy circles over that bundle of nerves. He was a master manipulator, strumming out perfect notes until I writhed and danced to his tune. I hated him; I wanted him. I needed more, everything he had to offer, and all the things I'd relish in prying from him. When he sank one finger inside me and pressed his thumb on my clit, I nearly came, biting down on my lip in an effort not to cry out.

The metallic tinge of blood coated my tongue along with mortification. I was going to come in front of all these people. The second my pussy started to clamp down on his finger, though, he stilled, leaving the sensation to fizzle away. Thank God. My body sagged at the reprieve, but he started right back up. And I wanted to scream for an entirely different reason. That was what he did through most of the main course—which I didn't touch. He kept me riding those waves, peaking and retreating until I was desperate. I didn't care who saw me anymore; I was just mindless with need. This was his punishment, I realized.

I could only imagine what I looked like right now, skin flushed, breaths uneven, his perfect little puppet, dancing on strings he plucked and pulled. And the worst part—he was barely even paying attention, carrying on a conversation as though he weren't completely wrecking me.

When I was beyond desperate, he finally turned to me. His breath caressed my throat, the skin feverish compared to the brush of his whiskey-chilled lips.

"You didn't make a sound." When his fingers left my body, a small whimper escaped me as though defying him on principle, and I felt him smile against my skin. "Good girl."

The praise made my insides tighten and clench, and Jesus Christ, I clearly had daddy issues.

He sat back in his chair, slipping that finger between his lips and sucking the taste of me from it. His eyes were all heat and drowning intensity, and in that moment, I wanted every bit of it. I wanted to taste myself on his tongue while he made me come for him. I'd never needed anything so much in my life. Anyone watching him would know exactly what he was doing, what he had done, but Giovanni didn't care because he was untouchable. And I didn't care because he'd made me mindless.

"So sweet. So pure and untouched." Then he fisted my hair and granted me my wish. He kissed me, his tongue slipping between my lips, forcing the combined taste of him and me and whiskey over my tongue.

That kiss re-ignited everything I was trying to simmer down until I was panting against his lips. Giovanni also seemed to have reached his limit because I was dragged to my feet and being led through the gala before I knew what was happening. My head spun from the alcohol and him and the lust pumping through my veins like a damn freight train.

The press of his hot palm on the bare skin of my back was a certain kind of torture in my heightened state. I felt as though every nerve ending had been singed and was now throbbing in rhythm with the pulse between my thighs.

It wasn't until Giovanni got behind the wheel of the fancy sports car that he no longer seemed so collected. He drove the stick into each gear like it had personally offended him. When we hit the interstate, his hand landed on my thigh like a brand, and I squirmed in response. My panties were damp, my thighs pressing together as though I could fix the ache he had put there. In public. The thought had a fresh wave of humiliation washing through me.

"I'm not your little toy to just play with in front of your rich friends," I snapped.

"You are whatever the fuck I say you are, Emilia." His fingers dug into my skin. "And right now, I say you're a brat, and brats get punished."

"What… what are you going to do?" I couldn't hide my trepidation.

The smile he shot my way was nothing short of wicked. "You'll see, princess."

My gaze drifted over him, and I didn't miss the bulge in his pants. My body was buzzing for him to finish what he had started in that ballroom. At the very least, I needed to be left alone so I could get myself off, but I had a feeling that he didn't walk out of a gala midway through the dinner just to take me home and leave me by myself. And that posed the question, did I want him to not leave me alone?

By the time we got into the apartment, I was desperate. I stumbled down the hall, more than ready to take care of this incessant fucking itch myself. Before I made it two steps, his hand was clamped on the back of my neck, holding me at his side as we walked. To my room. The moment that door closed behind him, his presence became oppressive and stifling in the four walls.

"What are you doing?"

He said nothing as he removed his jacket, just like he had that first night. But this time, there was zero fear, and my entire body coiled tight with the action. The cufflinks went next, his movements unhurried as though he had all the time in the world. Was he going to fuck me? For the first time since he'd taken me from that motel room, I couldn't quite convince myself that I didn't want it. By the time he had loosened the bowtie and rolled up his shirt sleeves, I'd backed into the corner, trying to rationalize with my sex-teased brain. I told myself I didn't want him, that he was the enemy, but it was like he'd drugged me with a dose of pure lust, and my gaze raked over every perfect inch of him like an addict needing my fix. The tux looked damn good on him, but this slightly rougher version…God, he was gorgeous. The crisp white shirt conflicted wildly with the dark and sinuous tattoos that crept just above his collar and encased both forearms like some secret treasure map just for me.

"Come here, piccola." He held a hand out to me, the devil inviting me to sell my soul.

But I wasn't that far gone. I remained against the wall, my palms pressed against the cool plaster as though I could sink my fingers in and anchor myself there.

"Are you scared, Emila?" He strolled forward a couple of steps.

"No."

"Or maybe you're just a little inebriated from the alcohol I warned you not to drink."

"I'm not a child," I said as he continued to edge closer, stalking his prey.

"No, you are not, but you have been a very bad girl."

Fuck. Why did my entire body hum at the sensual dip in his voice? Maybe I *was* drunk.

"It's time for your punishment." Would he hurt me? Fuck me? Both at the same time? "I warned you, Emilia."

He stopped in front of me, fingers winding around my throat in a way I would never admit I liked. His lips twitched when I whimpered, and he tugged me closer. "Don't be scared, piccola. I won't hurt you," he breathed over my cheek. "Much." Nothing about that whispered threat should have excited me.

His grip slipped to the back of my neck, and he wrenched me away from the wall. Toward the bed.

Panic cut through the fog of lust, and I fought him. "Giovanni, stop. What are you doing?"

He took a seat on the edge of the mattress and forced me over his lap. He pinned me there by the back of my neck, my hips over his thighs, ass in the air. My fingers gripped his calf, fighting and clawing to push upright and get away from him. He wrenched both arms behind my back before something silky wrapped around my wrists, binding them in the small of my back in such a way that I couldn't move. I felt like a kill ready to throw on a spit. I'd never been so physically vulnerable and to him of all people.

"Giovanni—'

"Shhh." His thumb stroked soft circles against the side of my throat as tears pricked my eyes. With his free hand, he dragged my skirt up my legs, but an orgasm was suddenly very far from my mind.

"Please," I whispered. I didn't even know what I was begging for, but this position was humiliating in the worst way.

"Take your punishment, piccola. And remember it next time you think to disobey me or run away again."

Cool air met my ass cheeks before a sharp crack rang out, followed by a sting across the back of my thigh. I cried out, more out of shock and sheer indignation than pain. He'd spanked me.

I started thrashing in his hold. "You can't do this!"

His grip on my neck tightened before his palm landed again and again. Heat tore over my butt cheeks, rivaling the inferno that was now my face. If he sought to humiliate me, he was doing a good job. I begged and pleaded, then demanded him to stop and pleaded some more, but he didn't quit. Blow after blow met my ass and thighs until everything hurt. A rabid kind of desperation rose in me, but it had nowhere to go, no outlet.

Finally, the part of me I clung to so hard, the part that fought and clawed and protected all my broken pieces, just crumbled. A sob of sheer despair choked me, and tears broke free as I went limp in his hold. His strikes changed, sweeping lower. Somewhere in the wreckage of my own mind, the pain numbed to something else. When I whimpered or remained still, he praised me, his fingers tracing over my pussy. And some warped corner of my mind craved his praise, his pleasure, the cruelty of his touch.

Suddenly, everything shifted, and the punishment didn't feel so punishing. Instead of trying to get away, I was pushing back, hoping he'd touch me where I really wanted. My submission was rewarded when he yanked my underwear to the side and plunged two fingers into my pussy. My mind checked out completely, leaving me with nothing more than instinct and sensations. I bucked and moaned on his lap, and he groaned in response.

"Such a tight, wet little pussy, princess. You like being spanked." His fingers slid in far too easily to deny it, and I was too far gone to feel the shame I normally would have. Again, Giovanni pushed me to the edge, only to back away.

I wanted to scream in frustration. I didn't think I could hate someone this much. Of all the things he'd done to me, this was the worst.

15

GIO

My dick was rock hard, pressing against Emilia's hip as she squirmed in my lap. My handprints branded her skin in a way I wished I could make permanent. This was supposed to be a simple case of dominating my little kitten, putting her back in her place, reminding her that she couldn't run from me. But I was losing myself in her every bit as much as she was lost to the sweet submission she didn't even understand.

Her perfect little pussy clamped around my fingers, trying to suck me deeper. I wanted to watch her fall apart and moan my name, preferably on my cock, but this was a punishment for her bratty ass. She'd only get my dick when she begged and gave me what I wanted. It almost hurt not to fuck her, though, so I inflicted my own suffering on her, edging her over and over until she was begging me to let her come.

"Please," she panted, voice cracking.

The little virgin was mindless, and I would keep her like that if I had to, tasting a world of pleasure her innocent mind couldn't even fathom before now. What she didn't know was that as powerless as she was supposed to be over my knee like this, she actually had all the power because the way she'd fractured and submitted so beautifully was driving me insane.

I released the tie from her hands and tossed her back on the bed. Fuck, she was gorgeous, chest heaving, hair wild, mascara streaking her face. She was always pretty, but she was a fucking goddess right now. This was her rawest, most pure form. No walls existed between us then, no hatred, no claws. It was just her and me. Lust and need.

The dress that made her the image of grace earlier in the evening was now rucked up around her waist, underwear shoved aside, pink pussy on display. She was temptation personified and she didn't even know it.

"Giovanni."

"Gio," I corrected her because only my enemies and my mother called me Giovanni.

"Gio."

I groaned. My name on her lips was like a fist around my throbbing dick.

Straddling her waist, I cuffed her wrists to the bed frame the same way I had last night. She stared up at me, pupils blown and lips parted, restrained. Fuck. She was so far gone, I knew she'd probably beg me to fuck her if I told her to, but I had to control myself. She was riding the tentative line between the mental and the physical right now. Too much, too soon, and all that vulnerability, that sweet trust, would disappear. And I wanted it, more than my next breath.

"This is your punishment, Emilia." I fisted the sheets as I bent to kiss her, needing to taste the tears on her lips, her desperation. "You don't get to come until you've learned your lesson."

"I have," she almost begged.

"And what is the lesson, Piccola?"

"I…not to run away?"

I smiled against her lips, though a flicker of anger sparked to life. "No. The lesson is that you're mine in every fucking way. I tell you not to drink the wine; you don't. You deny that you're mine…there are consequences. You run and put yourself at risk…"

Her breath hitched. "I'm sorry." She wasn't, though. Tomorrow, when she wasn't high as fuck on endorphins and hormones, she'd try and run again. Set a fire, stab me…who knew what she'd come up with next. Fighting was in her nature, and it was the very thing that drew me to her. And this dance of crime and punishment was one I would thoroughly enjoy with her, over and over again.

"You will be my wife, Emilia. Even if you haven't come to terms with it yet." I pulled back, rising to my knees over her and unfastening my belt. The second I fisted my dick, her gaze was locked on it. I stroked hard and fast, my balls already about to blow after watching her writhe and scream for the last hour.

Her innocent curiosity was so hot, and when her tongue flashed over her lips as though she wanted a taste, I was done. I might have teased her, but I'd tortured myself just as much. With a groan, I came, spurting ropes of it over her throat and chest, some landing on her skin, some soaking into the satin of her dress. There was a moment where we both just stared at each other, our rapid breaths filling the room. She was stunning like this, covered in my come. Mine.

I pushed to my feet and fastened my pants. When I adjusted her underwear, a whimper slipped past her lips. She was so sensitive, I knew I'd barely have to touch her to make her come right now.

"Please," she whispered.

I kissed her forehead. "Bad girls don't get to come, piccola." Then I tugged her dress down and moved to the bathroom. When I came back with a glass of water and some Tylenol, she frowned at me, anger creeping across that lust-blown gaze. "Open."

She hesitated before opening for me. She was learning. I placed the Tylenol on her tongue, fighting a growl when her lips closed around my fingers. Then I cupped the back of her head as I held the glass to her mouth.

"Drink it all, princess."

She did, and I set the glass on the side before sweeping my fingers over her cheek.

"Good girl."

She might be pissed, but she'd thank me in the morning when she didn't have a pounding headache and a throbbing ass. I pushed to my feet and made my way to the door.

"Gio, please. Don't leave me like this." She tugged at the restraints, her head thrashing back against the pillows, defenseless and covered in my come. I knew I was sick for liking the sight so much.

"We both know if I untie you, you'll get yourself off. And like I said, bad girls don't get to come, piccola."

Then I left.

There was no way I was sleeping after that, so I went to my office and poured a glass of whiskey while I watched her on the camera. Bound and writhing with frustration. My dick hardened again as I thought about how she'd finally submitted. Finally. And now she was so helpless, so beautiful in red satin and come. My own personal obsession.

I downed half the bottle of whiskey, watching, always fucking watching. Her breaths evened out, sleep finding her despite having her hands tied to the bed.

I swear, the text from Jackson was the only thing that stopped me from going in there and fucking her. Deal or no deal. Begging or not.

I fastened my shirt buttons and made my way downstairs. The cool night air wrapped around me, clearing the haze of primal need from my brain.

Jackson's SUV idled at the curb outside my building, the late-night traffic trickling on past. He and Tommy sat in the front, their expressions serious. That was enough to finally burst the bubble of bliss Emilia had created. I got into the back, and they both turned to look at me.

"This better be good."

Jackson eyed me up and down with a smirk. "Told you. He was totally balls deep."

I flipped him off, annoyed that I was, in fact, *not* balls deep.

"The Irish punchbag we had in the basement is dead."

"Okay. Did he give you anything?"

"Not exactly."

Tommy let out a strained sigh, flashing Jackson a look of disapproval. "He didn't say anything. But it turns out, he was Shane O'Hara." He lifted a brow. "Paddy's nephew."

Shit. War was war, and men died. Though I felt each loss keenly, family was different. It warranted retribution.

"Do they know we had him?" I asked.

Tommy nodded. "How do you think I found out it was him? O'Hara has offered a bounty for whoever took him."

I stared through the windshield at the glittering skyscrapers that towered around us. "Then we own it. Send the body back as a message. Keep taking our drugs and this is what happens."

Jackson smirked, and I wondered, not for the first time, if anything bothered him. "Want me to sew his fingers back on first?"

Tommy clipped him around the back of the head.

They would retaliate, and O'Hara wouldn't be coming for my soldiers. He'd be coming for my family, and these two and Nero were the closest thing I had anymore. And the woman I had just publicly declared as my fiancée…

I threw open the back door. "I'll go see Nero in the morning and warn him. Put a halt on everything again except the Pérez shipments."

"Rafe won't—"

"Fuck Rafe right now. We have Paddy O'Hara out for blood, and we can't do shit until we get this rat." The mob would always be three steps ahead until I found whoever it was. "Find him." And when we did, I was going to make a motherfucking ordeal out of his death. I stepped out onto the quiet sidewalk and went back to the penthouse. The sexual tension that had been drowning me had now ebbed away in the face of that violent dose of reality, and I went to bed.

A scream tore me from sleep. The glowing red numbers on the clock read two in the morning. Another shrill scream and I was up, grabbing the gun from the nightstand and palming it. I stepped into the hall and tiptoed my way to Emilia's room, quietly pushing open the door, half expecting to find some Outfit fuck trying to kill her. And maybe they were…in her dreams. The light from the TV screen was enough to highlight her thrashing form and the slight sheen of sweat that covered her bound body.

Placing the gun on the dresser, I took a seat on the edge of the bed and touched her arm. "Emilia."

Her eyes snapped open, and then she was trying to get away from me, but she couldn't because she was still tied to the bed. In her half-lucid state, she panicked, fighting and pulling, her breaths coming in ragged pants. I'd seen her in the throes of a nightmare on camera before, but this was different.

"Emilia, stop."

She didn't, and I had to physically pin her down to be able to free her. She was shaking and crying by the time the cuffs fell from her wrists, and when she tried to scramble away, I yanked her into my arms. Her attempts to fight me off were weak and half-hearted, as though whatever stalked her dreams had stolen her fire. I suspected it had more to do with her punishment than the nightmare itself. I felt the moment she submitted to me. It was perfect. Almost fucking spiritual. But she'd dropped a wall, some vital barrier, and it didn't surprise me that her demons were taking full advantage.

The hard set of her shoulders slowly softened, and she burrowed her face into my throat, tears wetting my skin. And I liked it because I wanted her at her darkest, her most broken. I wanted every single part of her, including those she didn't yet know, and the ones I would unleash. But most of all, I wanted the vulnerability she never showed.

"Breathe, piccola. It's just a nightmare." My fingers swept through the silky strands of her hair as the scent of my shampoo clung to them. Another way I'd marked her.

I was waiting, braced for the anger that was always simmering in her, but it never came.

"Sleep, princess." I pulled her down onto the bed and tucked her against my side.

She didn't fight or argue, and that was worrying. As was the fact that she let me hold her long after her tears had stopped wetting my chest. I wasn't sure if it was a gift or a curse because my little kitten was so very broken right then. I had to wonder what kind of demons could steal her spirit from her.

16

EMILIA

I woke to the dim light of my glorified prison cell, a low pounding ringing through my skull. It took me a few groggy seconds to notice the thick arm around my waist and the hot, heavy weight of a body pressed to my back. Giovanni. Memories of last night assaulted me, and I wrenched away from him, nearly falling out of the bed before stumbling to my feet.

He sat up, hair messy, sheets pooling at his hips. I hated that he looked so hot and well-rested and sated from jerking off on me. Meanwhile, I stood here in the stupid dress he'd made me wear, covered in his come, exhausted from the nightmares and strung tight enough to snap. He'd spanked me, tied me to a bed, and then held me while I cried. And I'd let him. *I let him.* In one night, Giovanni had left me more emotionally exposed than I'd ever been, but not by choice. It was a violation of the worst kind.

"Get the fuck out."

He cocked a brow, and I wanted to slap that sexy smirk off his face. "You don't want me to get out, Emila."

"I hate you," I whispered, the words sounding far more broken and strangled than I wanted.

"Because I punished you? Or because you're mine?"

"I'm not fucking yours!"

"You wanted to be mine last night." That smirk grew into a smile, and he lay back on the bed, folding his arms behind his head. His gaze flicked to my chest, to where he had come on me. "And you sure as hell look like mine right now."

I wanted to hurt him, to make him feel as powerless as I had been because I was so tired of men controlling me. He was right, though; I had begged him to make me come, wanted him, and that made it all so much worse. He'd manipulated me, twisted me up, and played me like the pawn I always fucking was.

Red mist descended, rage consuming me until I wanted to hurt him, but I couldn't because he was untouchable. Before I knew it, I was launching the lamp at a wall, porcelain scattering across the floor. Then I was tearing one of the TVs from the wall. "Controlling, psychopathic, asshole." It crashed to the floor, and the destruction was so satisfying, feeding the angry creature that now writhed beneath my skin. Then I turned the nightstand over, annoyed that he didn't have more decorative shit in here to trash. I was so intent on my rampage that I didn't even notice him move until he was standing right in front of me, looking better than he had any right to in just a pair of boxers. That pissed me off even more. The only small solace I found was in the dressing taped to his side, but even knowing I had cut him wasn't enough to temper me.

"Emilia…"

My hands slammed against his chest, and he just let me. Something in me was wide open, a gaping void of ugly pain and crippling weakness that was suddenly spilling out. I couldn't control it because I couldn't control anything. Tears broke free as my fists pounded against him, and his complete lack of reaction only enraged me further.

"You're all the same! At least my uncle or my father never tied me to a bed, though, so congratulations, Gio. You're officially the worst person I've ever met."

"You earned that punishment, piccola, and you know it."

"Because I want a life away from your bullshit mafia?"

"You'll never escape the mafia—mine or your uncle's. Blood in, blood out, and you were born with that blood in your veins."

A humorless laugh slipped from my throat. "So, what? This is my lot, and I should just lay down and play your sex slave?"

"Seemed pretty keen for my dick last night. Don't pretend otherwise."

My palm met his cheek with a resounding clap. His face twisted to the side before he smiled. Fucking smiled while the pink outline of my fingers blossomed on his skin. He was probably dreaming of all the ways he could punish me again, but I was past fear.

"You're just mad I didn't let you come."

"Fuck you, Gio." I went to hit him again because I wanted a damn reaction. I got one.

With a growl, he caught my wrist, then the other, binding them behind my back with one hand. I thrashed in his hold as he wrenched me against his near-naked body.

His grip on my wrists tightened as his other hand trailed down my chest, over the remnants of his dried come on my body. "Or maybe you're just pissed that I marked you. You look so beautiful like this, piccola."

My skin heated, his touch a curse I couldn't fight.

"So tainted. So angry."

"Don't touch me," I breathed, closing my eyes.

He made me crave things I didn't want to. It was like I didn't even recognize myself.

"Please."

He didn't release me.

"We both know you want me to touch you, to make you come. On my fingers. My tongue. My cock."

My entire body trembled with need as his lips whispered over my cheek, but it wasn't real, just a manipulation.

"But you aren't handling your submission very well right now."

"That was not submission—"

"And as much as I like seeing you covered in me…" He released me and stepped back. "Get in the shower, princess."

I frowned at him, confused and reeling.

"Don't worry. Soon enough, I'll mark you much more permanently." One finger brushed my throat. "My grip imprinted on your throat, my come in that tight pussy, my name..."

I stumbled away from him, part sick at the thought and part curious. That damn curiosity was going to cost me.

"Shower. Now."

I suddenly felt numb, drained, and my feet seemed to move on their own. When I went into the bathroom, he followed, his bare feet padding over the tile.

"What are you—"

He cut on the shower, then stepped in front of me. "Take off your dress, Emilia."

I jerked away from him with a glare. "Gio, I am not—"

"Take off the damn dress before I do it for you."

"Fuck you."

He closed his eyes and pinched the bridge of his nose on a hard sigh. My gaze strayed to his flexed bicep, the tension that gripped every muscle.

"I'm trying to help you, princess. For once, just trust me." Trust him? The idea was ridiculous. Wasn't it?

"Why would I trust you?" I whispered.

His gaze met mine, cool and steady. "Because I know what you need, and I'm going to give it to you."

"I don't want you—"

"Dress, Emilia." It was a command given by a man who was used to being obeyed.

The silence that descended between us seemed even more punctuated by the hammering of the water over the tile behind me. My lungs felt too tight, the bathroom too small.

"One."

When he held up a finger, every fiber of my being screamed with indignation. And yet there was this part of me, a part that had been so brutally exposed last night that trusted him, that wanted to obey.

"What happens if you get to three?" I breathed, and I knew those words were a red rag to a bull the second they left my lips.

His eyes flashed. "Bad girls don't get to come, piccola."

I sucked in a shaky breath, a little thread of excitement cutting through all the rage that I was so desperately trying to hold onto. Was I really going to do this? The urge to rebel against him warred with the need to just stop thinking and fighting, just to feel. Giovanni was a high that made me forget my bleak reality for a moment, and as his eyes met mine, he promised me oblivion without uttering a single word.

With shaky fingers, I reached for my zip, the sound of it lowering like a gunshot cutting through the room. I wasn't sure either of us was breathing as I toed this tentative line between lust and fury. The material slipped from my shoulders and pooled at my feet, leaving me in only my thong and the bandage at my thigh. I'd never been naked in front of a man, never been so exposed—physically or emotionally— as I was with him in that moment. Cool air kissed my nipples, and they peaked under his heated gaze. Gio let out a small groan, backing against the vanity, giving me space.

"Now the panties, piccola." His voice was a deep rasp, and any reticence I might have felt was chased away by the look of pure want on his face.

As I slid the scrap of lace down my legs, his knuckles whitened on the edge of the vanity as though he were physically holding himself in place.

"Get in the shower," he said through gritted teeth.

I did, stepping under the warmth of the water. Only when the glass door closed did he move, like he needed a shield between us. I felt like prey, trapped in a cage with a monster prowling outside the bars, waiting to eat me.

His fierce gaze burned into me through the misting glass. "Spread your legs, piccola."

Embarrassment crept in, and I hesitated. I'd never been naked in front of him, yet he wanted me to spread my legs so he could see *every*thing… He cocked a brow and held up two fingers when I didn't immediately comply. I glared at him, even as a rush of anticipation thrummed through my veins.

"Let me see that pretty pink pussy."

Fuck, why were his dirty words so hot? The glass between us misted further, and I knew he couldn't see me clearly. Was that deliberate? It allowed me a little courage, and I spread my legs.

"Good girl."

Those two words were like a Tazer to my need, and I was right back to last night, desperate to please him, desperate for his touch. "Gio…"

His palm pressed to the glass, his other hand sliding down his body, over each raised ab. "Touch yourself for me, Emilia."

I hated doing as I was told, but the need to come reignited, as though last night had never stopped. There was something in the way he commanded me that made it so much better than just getting myself off.

When my fingers brushed between my legs, I couldn't fight the whimper that escaped me.

"Circle that clit for me, princess," Gio ordered on a ragged groan.

I could barely see him now, but that sound made me want to, need to. Swiping my hand over the glass, I cleared it enough that I could see his boxers shoved down, fist gripping his thick cock. He looked feral, out of control, his frenzy feeding my own. My free hand pressed against his on the other side of the glass, as though I could touch him, feel him.

He grunted, breaths quickening along with my own as I did what he said. I was so close, teetering on the ledge he left me clinging to last night. Only now it felt so much higher, like the fall would be endless. But now I was in control, or so I thought.

"Slide two fingers into that pussy, piccola."

I did, and the orgasm I was teetering on withdrew, but it was replaced with a different kind of pleasure, a burn and stretch that made me crave the rough thickness of the fingers he'd fucked me with last night.

"Good girl. Feel how wet and tight you are for me. Imagine how good it'll feel when I fuck you." His voice stroked over my senses, painting a filthy picture in my mind.

I swiped the glass once more and stared at him, stroking his cock, imagining what it would feel like to have him inside me.

"Now press your thumb over your clit. Just like I would if I were touching you right now."

I did, and a moan fell from my lips. I'd made myself come before, but this was different. The sight of Gio frantically stroking his dick had me hurtling toward something monumental.

"Emila," he growled my name. "Come for me."

And I did, my entire body detonating as I watched him snarl and jerk, shooting come over his hand and stomach. Giovanni Guerra losing control over me was the sexiest thing I'd ever seen, and it made me feel empowered in a way I never had before.

A heady kind of pleasure tore through me, stealing every bit of strength from my limbs. He wasn't touching me, but he might as well have been because with that orgasm, it felt like he was rearranging all my pieces into something I no longer recognized.

I staggered back against the shower wall, gasping for breath. Gio's gaze met mine through the half blurry swipe I'd left on the glass, and I suddenly felt like an exposed nerve. Hot then cold and feeling every single thing. When he opened the door and stepped inside, I froze.

I was caught between secretly wanting more yet terrified of him and everything he represented. I was so scared of letting go and losing even more of the control he stripped me of so easily. Control that I had surrendered to him the second I had lowered the zipper on that dress.

Gio made no move to touch me, simply stepped under the spray and washed the come from his stomach. I remained against the wall, a silent voyeur to his casual calm. I couldn't even find it in me to be ashamed of my nakedness, of what we had just done, because he was so blatantly *un*ashamed.

Water poured over his golden skin, tattoos warping and dancing in the flow, muscles popping and rolling with each subtle movement. God, he was like art.

At some point, he'd removed the dressing on his ribs, the neat stitches bisecting the image of a lion on his skin. In a messed up way, I wanted to scar him because he'd already scarred me, physically and emotionally.

"You're bleeding."

I snapped out of my staring and followed his gaze to my feet, where the water was tinged pink. I must have cut my foot on the smashed lamp. "I'm fine."

He got out without a word while I lingered beneath the spray, trying to put myself back together. By the time I stepped out of the stall, I had expected Gio to be long gone. Instead, he was there, offering me a towel. I took it and wrapped myself up as though it could shield me from him. From this. But I couldn't stop staring at his bare chest or tracing that drop of water that trickled all the way over every damn ab before meeting the towel at his waist.

"If you're done looking at me like dessert…"

My face went up in flames, and laughter rang around the room as he grabbed my waist and placed me on the vanity like a child.

"What are you—"

He took a first aid kit from the cabinet and dropped to one knee, placing my foot on his thigh. The pristine white of his towel was instantly tainted with a slash of crimson.

"Gio, I'm fine." Embarrassment finally wormed its way through whatever haze he'd put me in. For last night, and my temper tantrum this morning, for what just happened in the shower, and the way he was taking care of me now—I didn't know how to deal with any of it. I just needed him to leave me alone to process it all and reconstruct the walls he'd torn down so easily. "I can take care of myself."

Long fingers clamped around my ankle when I tried to pull away. "For once in your life, Emilia, just stop fighting."

I snapped my mouth shut, and he inspected my foot, then bandaged it. This was becoming a habit with us. Just as I thought that, he pushed to his feet and reached for the wet bandage around my thigh, removing it and inspecting the wound.

"It looks good."

I didn't know what to say. I could barely look at him. I pushed to my feet, and he gripped my jaw, sweeping his thumb across my cheekbone that I knew must have been stained pink.

"So fucking innocent, piccola." His lips twitched before his hand fell away. "It's still early. You should go back to sleep."

"I won't be able to."

He tilted his head as though waiting for me to elaborate, and before I knew it, I was doing just that.

"The lack of windows…it makes the nightmares worse," I mumbled. I felt stupid saying that, like I was some little girl afraid of the dark. "When I used to run away, my father would lock me in the basement for a couple of days as punishment." Why I admitted that, I didn't know. Maybe I just wanted him to know that I wasn't totally pathetic. That there was a reason.

"He did what?" His voice became eerily quiet, and I imagined that was how he sounded when he ordered someone's death.

"I…not like that." I dropped my gaze to the floor, wishing a hole would open up and swallow me. "It wasn't a dungeon or anything. Just…isolated. And without windows."

There was a beat of silence before Gio cleared his throat. "You can sleep in my bed."

My gaze snapped to his, but before I could refuse, he cut me off.

"I've got work to do anyway."

Then he left, and I could do nothing but ask myself what the hell had just happened.

17

GIO

The thought of Emilia in my bed proved too much. I had to go see Nero anyway, so I left the apartment before the sun had fully risen. The first red hues of dawn reflected off the water as I crossed the bridge out of the city, the harsh notes of Metallica thrumming through my speakers in a vain attempt to chase away my tiredness.

Things were about to get ugly with the mob, and I should have been focused on that, yet my mind kept drifting to Emilia. I asked myself, for what felt like the hundredth time, why the hell I was doing this with her. Why her? What was so special about this one girl that I couldn't just let it go? I couldn't answer *that* any more than I could do the smart thing and send her back. I just couldn't. A situation I was supposed to be in complete control of was now very much out of control and in the hands of a girl who had no idea the power she truly wielded.

When I pulled up to the enormous glass mansion that was Nero's Hamptons house, his guards let me in. Unlike my own house, his was quiet. He didn't need men here to keep it safe.

The thought was laughable. I stepped into the kitchen and caught sight of their housekeeper, Margot, at the stove, just as the barrel of a gun kissed the base of my skull. Margot just smiled and shook her head like this was so amusing.

I let out a sigh. "Una."

Nero's wife stepped in front of me, a baby propped on her hip as she holstered the weapon at her thigh. Dressed in all black, she looked like she was about to go full tac team. She probably was. If Nero was scary, then Una was terrifying, even with Tatyana on her hip. Individually, their reputations were bloody. Together, Nero and Una were the stuff of nightmares. I could never quite bring myself to trust the Russian assassin, no matter how long she was with my best friend.

"Why are you in my house, Gio?"

"I need to see Nero."

"He's getting Dante up. I have to go." The "kill someone" was unspoken. She kissed the baby's head and thrust her at me.

I grabbed her reflexively, staring into wide indigo eyes the exact same strange color as her mother's.

"Tell Nero she's been changed and fed."

Margot handed her a to-go coffee mug, and Una scooped up a black holdall that was undoubtedly full of weapons before slipping out the door. Meanwhile, Tatyana was staring at me like I was the definition of stranger danger. I took a seat at the kitchen table and rocked her while I waited. For a moment, a sense of peace washed over me. She was so innocent, so utterly pure and untouched by the atrocities of the world.

"Careful. You look a little too comfortable there." Nero's voice had my gaze snapping up. Gone was his usual suit, and in its place was a T-shirt and workout pants. He was no less intimidating with his height and bulk, but it was just...weird. I could never correlate Nero, the ruthless mafia boss I'd known my entire life—even before he was actually boss— with this version of him.

"Jesus. You're one kid off a dad bod," I said with a smirk.

He flipped me off. "I can still kick your ass. Want a demonstration?"

I grinned. "Can't. I'm holding the baby."

Dante barrelled into the room like a tornado of toddler chaos, all wild black curls and Una's eyes staring back at me. The kid was only three, and I swear to God, he had the devil in him.

"Gio." He looked so damn happy to see me, though I knew what he was after. He stopped beside my chair, and I plucked the bag of candy from my pocket, handing it off like it was a damn shakedown. Just like that, he bolted for the door.

Nero caught him by the back of his shirt. "Not before breakfast, Dante."

I laughed as my friend glared at me. "You're a dick."

"Dick!" Dante announced, and I threw my head back on a laugh.

Nero wrestled Dante into a high chair, forcibly bending his legs when he acted like he had rigor mortis. The whole scene was so weird and yet so normal that for a minute, I was bitterly jealous. Nero was a mafia boss married to a Russian assassin, but they had a slice of bliss here, something away from blood, money, and power. Something more important. This was what he took a step back for, and it was so worth it.

I pictured this with Emilia, imagined her with my child. For a second, I wanted it so fucking badly that it was almost painful. Then I blinked, and reality resumed. I had problems to deal with, shit to focus on.

"Come on. Bring my princess." Nero grabbed two coffees while Margot put a bowl of oatmeal in front of Dante that I was sure they'd both be wearing soon enough.

We went into the living room, and I took in the cream furniture and crystal chandelier. He hadn't changed the place much since he had taken it from his father, and I didn't understand why. Not like he was close with Cesare. He'd killed the man and taken his place, for fuck's sake.

Nero placed the drinks down before taking Tatyana from me. I actually missed her small weight in my arms. Nero cocked a brow at me as he placed her on his shoulder.

"Are you…" he narrowed his eyes, "broody?"

"Don't be ridiculous."

He laughed and picked up his coffee. "Well, according to *The Times*, you're engaged now."

"That was just for appearances."

"With the girl that you agreed to marry in exchange for an Outfit alliance? That was just for appearances…"

He took a seat in the armchair, and I dropped onto the couch.

"It's… She's…" Fuck, how was I going to explain my deal with Emilia?

"She ran. You don't want to force her, but they also tried to kill her, so you aren't sending her on her merry way." He took a sip of coffee while rubbing over Tatyana's back, his hand spanning her entire body. "You're predictable as fuck, Gio."

"And Jackson and Tommy gossip like old women."

"Tommy gossips with Una."

"And Una gossips with you."

"The Kiss of Death does not *gossip*." He snorted. "She passes on useful information."

I traced one finger over a shaft of sunlight on the arm of the chair, not wanting to look at him while I spoke about Emilia. It felt too…weak, maybe. "You aren't going to tell me that I'm being stupid and I should send her back or bathe in her blood."

He shrugged one large shoulder, Tatyana bobbing with the movement. "Tommy said she'd be good for you. You could do with a little good." It was almost…nice for Nero. If only that little good actually wanted me, though.

"You didn't come to talk about your future wife, though. What brings you here, aside from the obvious?" He reclined back in his seat, and even in this casual state, with a baby on his chest, Nero radiated power.

"I came to warn you. We caught some mob kid with a stolen shipment. Jackson did his thing. Killed him."

He lifted a brow. "Did he find the rat?"

"No."

His slow release of breath seemed to ratchet the tension in the room. I knew he was pissed because if there were two things Nero valued most, it was loyalty and fear, and the fact that anyone would be brave enough to betray him infuriated him.

"Turns out the kid was Shane O'Hara. Patrick's nephew."

The smile that crept over Nero's lips tinged on insanity. Mad fucker. "Paddy's gonna be pissed."

"Yeah, he's going to want retribution."

Nero cracked his neck to the side. "Good. Let's get this shit done. Call Jackson. We'll go wipe out the mob tonight." He pushed to his feet, and I followed, standing in front of him.

"You know that'll fuck us over in the long run. We have a good thing going with Rafe and Chicago. We're untouchable in New York because we keep the dirty shit there." Years; I had worked for years to get all the pieces lined up on the board. No one liked attention, and taking out the entire mob…that drew the kind of attention that had blowback. "We start a blood bath and that bubble of protection disappears."

"You just said they're about to come at us. I didn't ask you to run my city just so you could tiptoe around this shit."

"No, you asked me to run things because you don't care for the bullshit politics required to run a business."

Tatyana started to fuss, and I had to smile at the sight of Nero going from homicidal to shushing the tiny thing.

"From what I hear, you're moving away from Rafe anyway."

I rolled my eyes. "No, I'm just not putting all our eggs in one basket. He won't ship anywhere but Chicago, and that has fucked us."

"Yeah, well, now he's up my ass, which means Anna and Una are up my ass, too. So, we handle this shit tonight, everything goes back to normal and my ass is safe."

"We both know you're about money and war, Nero. Well, I make you money. War will fuck that. And more importantly, it's a risk. You have a family…."

His brows pulled together, and I knew he hated it. Hated that he had to temper who he was to protect what he loved. But Nero and Una had seen enough blood and death to last a lifetime. They may not have been people who appreciated the quiet, but they needed it.

I clapped a hand on his shoulder. "Just watch your back, and keep Rafe off mine a little longer. If it goes south and I need the big guns, you know I'll call you." I stroked a finger over Tatyana's downy hair, tempted to demand he hand her over before I left. I wouldn't give him any ammo, though. "Look after them." I turned toward the door. "Oh, and Una said the baby has been fed and changed." I laughed as I walked out of his house. From war to babies in a heartbeat. That was his life now, and fuck, I thought I might want it.

I stopped in at my own house while I was up here. It was mid-morning by the time I arrived, and there were more men there than usual. Jackson having put out the call last night for them to come in. Out on the streets, alone, soldiers could be picked off too easily, and I wasn't about to hand O'Hara bodies. The kitchen was a hive of energy, the scent of coffee and pastry filling the air. And I didn't miss Renzo Donato sitting beside Tommy at my kitchen table. He looked so much like Emilia, and for the briefest moment, guilt flickered at the edges of my consciousness.

The kid hadn't done anything wrong except try to protect his sister. Wouldn't I have done the same thing for my sister? My only sister was older and married off long before I could have done anything about it. But the old Famiglia would not allow their daughters to be abused in arranged marriages. The Outfit evidently had no such qualms based on how easily Sergio had handed Emilia over. *Fuck her, marry her, I don't care.*

Still, Renzo was an Outfit enforcer, and he had stolen my bride and helped her run—for four days.

"Tommy, why is Sergio Donato's nephew wandering my house?" I picked up some mail on the counter and shuffled through it.

"Jackson was using the cell. I figured you'd rather have Renzo in a guest room than the Irish fucker. Less blood on the sheets."

I glanced at him as he smiled around his coffee mug.

"Besides, isn't he technically going to be your brother-in-law soon?"

Renzo glared at me like I was the devil himself.

"You do anything, and not only will you go right back in that blood-stained cell, but your sister will pay for it," I warned.

Tommy snorted. "Trust me, after seeing her in that dress last night, there's no way he's touching your sister in any way she doesn't like."

And now Renzo looked like he'd kill me if he could. I couldn't help but smile.

"I thought we were supposed to be 'allies.'" He said it mockingly as though the entire notion were a joke.

"Do you see me wearing a wedding ring, Donato?" I skimmed over a letter about some city meeting.

"No."

"Correct. So, we are not family. And that makes you a potential enemy, sitting at my fucking table."

He stopped talking, shoving a mouthful of food in his face.

"I'm surprised you left The Outfit princess alone," Jackson said as he came in and passed me, shoving a mug beneath the coffee machine. "I hear she stabbed you, then tried to burn your apartment down, and almost escaped last night."

"Emilia is nothing if not tenacious." My gaze met Renzo's smug one. "She was punished, though." I imagined he pictured all kinds of horrible things when his smile fell. Least of all, me spanking and coming on his little sister. "No need to look so murderous, Renzo. Nothing her bratty little ass didn't secretly like."

Jackson chuckled just as my phone rang. "Speak of the devil," I said as I stepped out into the hall.

"Sergio."

"O'Hara just took out four of my guys at a café in broad fucking daylight." Shit. It had started. "Want to tell me what the hell is going on?"

"Let's just say one of our mutual friend's favorite pets had to be put down."

"For fuck's sake." A few more curses followed. "I'm coming to New York. We need to meet."

"Fine. Eight o'clock. The Yama in Desolation." Desolation was neutral ground. I sure as shit couldn't go to Chicago right now.

———

Emilia was tense in the passenger seat as I inched through heavy traffic, her gaze fixed on the passing bustle of the New York streets. The black dress she wore clung to her curves perfectly, and I struggled to pay attention to the road.

Today had been a shitshow, with O'Hara taking out two of my own guys in Chicago. My mood was black, and yet in a sea of death and chaos, Emilia was like this shaft of pure white light that I wanted to bask in. Even if I couldn't right now. She absentmindedly twirled my mother's ring around her finger in what I surmised was a nervous tick.

"Where are we going?" she asked as we finally made it onto the bridge and headed out of the city.

"To a meeting." I didn't elaborate and tell her who it was with or why.

Sergio had tried to kill her, and I didn't want fear driving her to do something stupid. Like run in the middle of Desolation. She'd be trafficked off the street in a heartbeat.

We fell into silence for the rest of the hour drive, and I gripped the steering wheel tight, the urge to touch her, to pull her from her head almost instinctual. But right now, I needed not to think about Emilia or marriage or any future past finding my rat and putting an end to this war. It had gone on too long, and with Shane O'Hara's death, this was one step away from becoming the kind of blood feud that would span generations.

I pulled onto the dirty streets of Desolation. The town sat a few miles outside New York, a messy collection of run-down apartment buildings and graffiti-stained, boarded-up shop fronts. The place was a sess pit of crime, run by the Ruin, a collection of crime lords who used it as neutral ground. Nero had been invited to join, but of course, he didn't play well with others. I parked in a side alley and helped Emilia out of the car. She looked around like someone was about to jump out and stab her.

"Don't look so scared, princess. I'll protect you."

She glared at me, smoothing a hand down the front of her dress. She looked out of place, a flower growing in a heap of shit. "Did you bring me to a meeting with your drug dealers?"

I laughed. "Not quite."

I released the gun from my chest holster and palmed it as we crossed the street to a nondescript-looking building. The sidewalk was littered with garbage, the odd homeless person rifling through it.

"Why have you really brought me here?" Her voice trembled slightly as she eyed the gun in my hand.

"I'm not about to kill you, Emilia." I rolled my eyes. "I told you, I have a meeting."

"So you say." She looked around like she might catch a disease simply from walking along the sidewalk. "For all I know, you're about to leave my body in a dumpster. This looks like a popular murder spot." She was rambling, though even as she spoke about me killing her, she shifted closer, her body pressing into my side.

My arm came around her, tugging her closer still. I liked the feel of her too much, liked that she gravitated to me for safety.

I stopped outside a plain black door with a single light above it, all the windows of the building boarded up. "I'd never kill you, princess." I rapped on the door. "You're worth much more to me alive."

She didn't get a chance to respond before the door opened, the low trickle of music drifting from within.

There was a small, dark room with a single desk and an older man in a suit behind it. I placed my gun on the desk, followed by the other still strapped to my chest. The guy put them in a safe at the back of the room before patting me down. He looked at Emilia, and I shook my head, daring him to try to touch her. Seemingly thinking better of it, he ducked and backed away while waving us toward the double doors at the back.

As soon as I stepped through those doors, the soft thrum of jazz music surrounded me. To the unsuspecting eye, The

Yama looked like a high-end club, a wild contradiction to its exterior. Velvet-lined booths and crystal chandeliers decorated the place, and groups of men and women alike gathered behind sheer curtains that gave an illusion of sordid mystery. Beautiful waitresses served drinks, leaving their guests wanting for nothing. This was a place where a man could have any fantasy fulfilled if he had enough money. But that was the pretty lie, hiding what lay beneath. The Yama was owned by the bratva, and in English, it meant pit. Right below our feet, in the bowels of the building, was a fighting ring. Men often spent more money betting on blood and violence than on whores. And The Pit offered no-holds-barred fights to sate even the most bloodthirsty. There was a time when Nero and Jackson had loved getting into that filthy ring. Before we became who we are. The entire place was a money-making machine, thriving on a man's basest desires.

Emilia stayed beside me, and I wanted to pull her close, but I didn't. The Yama was a nest of vipers, full of the kind of men who could become an enemy at any time. It was never wise to show dangerous people your weakness. To the world, she was my fiancée, a Donato, an arranged bride whom I should have zero attachment to. But to anyone who dared look closely, Emilia was a soft spot.

We cut through the club, winding through barely clothed waitresses and dancers. I knew the second Emilia spotted Sergio and his companion sitting in the booth at the back because she slammed to a halt, heels digging in before she stumbled backward.

"Emilia—"

"You're giving me to them?" She sounded so hurt, so betrayed, so fucking scared.

For a moment, I forgot all about pretenses and weakness, cupping her face in both hands, right there in the middle of the club where anyone could see. "No, piccola. This is a business meeting. I brought you because it's not safe right now, and I want you with me."

I didn't elaborate on the fact that she might be in more danger with me. It was selfish, but at least I could think clearly while I could see her. A rat had made it to my upper ranks. I wanted to trust my men, but the simple fact was, no one would protect her like I would.

"Then why is Matteo here?" Her gaze darted around as though she were looking for an escape. She was in full flight mode.

"I don't know who—"

"Please don't let them take me, Gio." Terror flickered through those murky-green eyes, and I swept my thumb over her cheekbone.

"Piccola, you know I'll keep you forever if you let me."

"Please." She trembled slightly, and I wanted to turn around and get her far away from these men, this so-called family who would do this to her. But I needed to speak to Sergio, and I wasn't letting her out of my sight.

When I had what I wanted, I would kill Sergio Donato for no other reason than he'd done something to scare her. She didn't need to know the lengths I would go to keep her, though. For a second, I didn't even care about our deal or the threat of her uncle that I was using as leverage.

"You're mine, Emilia. He won't touch you. I promise."

She blinked until the glassy sheen of tears in her eyes retreated. I glanced over to where Sergio watched us with rapt interest. The man beside him, however, was glaring like I'd just taken a shit in his cornflakes.

Emilia finally nodded, and I dropped my hands from her face and threaded my fingers with hers.

"Come. This won't take long."

Her grip on my hand tightened as we approached the table, expression shuttering into something totally unreadable. Emilia was guarded, but I could always see each and every emotion playing out on her face. She was passionate and volatile and even vulnerable at times, but I barely recognized the version she presented to her uncle now. The wild creature I had captured was nowhere to be seen, and she was every bit the stoic mafia princess. She didn't want them to witness her fear. Good girl. I squeezed her hand.

The man seated beside Donato was younger, perhaps my age, but with the same slimy air around him that said he'd kill his own grandmother if it served him. He dragged a hand over buzzed, dark hair, gaze raking over Emilia in a way that made my fingers twitch for my gun.

"Ah, Guerra." Sergio pushed to his feet when we approached, and I shook his offered hand when I'd rather cut off his fingers. "And you brought my niece. What a pleasant surprise." His beady eyes bounced between Emilia and me. "This is Matteo Romano, my consigliere."

I shook the other man's hand before Sergio pulled Emilia forward and kissed both her cheeks. She made no attempt to touch him, her entire body rigid in his embrace. *He tried to kill her.* I took a deep breath to calm myself, pulling Emilia back to my side. When Romano moved toward her, she pressed into me, recoiling against my body. The man smirked slightly, enjoying her reaction. It took every ounce of willpower not to slam his face into the table right then and there. But violence was not tolerated here in the club, and I wanted this meeting over with already.

Emilia sat beside me, but I knew she wanted to bolt.

"You look well, Emilia," Sergio said. "Wouldn't you agree, Matteo?"

The other man's gaze slipped over her, and she stared back at him cooly. "Yes, you've always been the shining gem of the Donato family, *Emi*."

She stiffened, and my arm slipped along the back of the booth, fingers trailing over her shoulder.

I was done with the bullshit. "You wanted to meet in person, Donato; here I am."

"Yes. Here you are. *You* took the O'Hara boy, and now my men are paying the price."

"Your men are cannon fodder, Donato. That's what you brought to the table."

His jaw clenched, a vein in his forehead visibly pulsing. "You starting a blood debt was not part of our agreement."

"Yes, well, there are plenty of things that were 'not part of our agreement.'" Like him trying to kill his own niece.

A beat of silence rang around the table, and I kept stroking over Emilia's skin, using it to calm myself as much as her. I would not show an outburst of emotion to this man.

"This is war, Sergio. Men die." The mob's, and The Outfit's anyway. My men were not supposed to die, though, and it cut me far deeper than I would ever let on.

"You lost two. I lost eight today alone, and who knows if that's the end of it. You killed his damn nephew."

I shrugged because I knew it was a cock-up, but this was the Famiglia. We apologized for nothing. The second a man apologized, he appeared weak and he opened himself up to attack.

A waitress brought a bottle of wine and poured four glasses before retreating.

Matteo's attention followed her half-naked ass before snapping right back to where it had been this entire conversation—on Emilia. He stared at her like a man who'd walked through the desert for a week and she was a glass of water.

I took a sip of the wine, wondering if Romano would scream like a little bitch if I smashed the glass and rammed the broken stem into his throat.

"I see you came to your senses, Emilia." Sergio nodded to the ring on Emilia's finger, and she paled. "I'm impressed you managed to tame her, Giovanni."

"There is a certain appeal in breaking the wild ones," Matteo said, still focused on my fiancée, salivating over her like a drooling dog.

My fingers tensed around the wine glass, and Emilia subtly leaned toward me. I let out a breath, tension ebbing away as the scent of my shampoo mixed with her sweet smell wafted over me. It was unlike her, and I wasn't sure if she just hated her uncle enough to present a united front, or Romano made her so uncomfortable that she sought out the safety of my presence.

"Mr. Romano, if you keep looking at my fiancée like that, you will find out exactly how I earned my reputation."

Sergio chuckled as though this was all a big game. "Now, now, as you know, I was going to give Emilia to another. You can forgive a man for looking at what he might have had."

My temper went nuclear in an instant, and as if she could feel it, Emilia grabbed my free hand under the table. She was fucking shaking, terrified, and it made me livid.

"There was no *might*." I glared at the man who thought he could have what was mine. "No possibility. Emilia is mine." I lifted her hand and brushed my lips over her fingers, over the ruby that sat pride of place.

Her gaze met mine, and though her mask was still in place, I could see it in her eyes, the cracks starting to form. When I looked back at Romano, he feigned a smile, but he couldn't hide the rage, the slight twitch of his eye. There was a man who felt he was owed something.

"Now, can we get back to business?"

"Yes." Sergio straightened. "I want to hit the mob with a coordinated attack in a few days. They killed my men, and I have no doubt they'll kill more in the coming days—yours and mine. Let's hit them hard."

This was a route I didn't want to go down, but I wasn't going to deny Sergio his need for blood. Nero had proposed the same plan. The difference being The Outfit would be the face of this, not us. "Fine. Jackson will work out the finer details."

Serio pushed to his feet. "I'm going to leave Matteo in New York to liaise. I trust he will be safe in your city." It was a loaded comment.

I looked from Sergio to Emilia. There was something about Matteo Romano that upset her. Could I promise his safety? Technically, I had started this with Shane O'Hara, so I didn't have a whole lot of choice.

"No one will kill him." It was the most I was going to offer.

I pulled Emilia to her feet beside me and shook Sergio's hand, once more ignoring Romano. The man was asking for a slit jugular. Emilia offered no goodbyes to either of them.

The moment we were out of sight of their table, she slipped from my hold and was practically running for the exit. Once outside, she moved away from me, tipping her face back to the sky for a minute.

"Emilia." I brushed her arm, and she flinched. "Talk to me, piccola."

"There's nothing to talk about." She started across the road to the car.

One thing was for sure, there was a lot to fucking talk about because the girl who had just sat silently through that meeting was not the person I'd spent the last week with.

The ride home was silent, the kind where each breath felt ominous. Emilia was so far inside her head, she might as well have been on a different continent, and I knew it had something to do with Romano. The way she reacted to him… I had to wonder what he had done to her, but that was a dark and dangerous path. One that would result in me breaking my word to Sergio.

I would allow her silence until we got home. But that was it. After last night, I realized my little kitten needed pushing. Emilia would never come to me "willingly." But she wanted to. Oh, how she wanted to. Nothing in this world could keep her from me, though, not even her pride. Emilia was on the verge of breaking, so I would push her, and I would catch all her shattered pieces and put them back together when she did.

W hen we got home, Emilia seemed lost, disjointed as she lingered in the space between the door and the kitchen.

I handed her a glass of water. "Drink that."

She did as she was told.

I put the empty glass on the counter before stroking her hair away from her face. "Go get in my bed, piccola. I have some calls to make." I pressed my lips to her forehead, and she leaned into me, placing her palms on my chest. I couldn't deny there was part of me that loved her sweet acceptance, but I was also concerned because even at her weakest, Emilia *always* fought me.

I went to my office and called Nero, then Jackson. By the time I was done, it was well past midnight. I could have gone and slept in one of the spare rooms. I should have, but I didn't.

Emilia was curled on her side in my bed, looking so small and fragile. She still wore her dress, her hair half pinned up. When I approached with a shirt in hand, her glazed eyes didn't move from the city beyond the windows.

"Sit up."

She did, like a robot being controlled. I stripped her out of her dress before slipping the shirt over her head. She was so meek, I couldn't even enjoy the sight of her in lace underwear.

"Emilia," I cupped her cheek and pulled her face to mine. She blinked, and a lone tear tracked down her cheek. "Talk to me."

Her mouth opened, then closed. "Why? We aren't friends, Gio."

Oh, we were so much more than that. "We don't have to be enemies."

"I think we do." Her words were a broken whisper. She needed us to be enemies because the moment she let me in, we both knew I'd consume her entirely.

"I'm not your enemy, Emilia, and if you really thought that, you wouldn't be in my bed."

She dropped her gaze to the sheets as though realizing the truth in my words.

"So tell me, who is Matteo Romano to you? And how much do I need to make him suffer when I kill him?"

She huffed a laugh that sounded more like a sob. More tears fell, and I watched her break. Those walls I'd battered myself against over and over again cracked as though they were made of nothing more than sand.

"Don't cry, piccola."

I lay down on the bed, fully clothed, and pulled her trembling form to my chest. Tears soaked through my shirt and onto my skin for the second time in as many days. And I wanted it— every tear, every shred of hurt, every fear that lived in her head. Those tears felt like a branding of her pain, like she was tattooing herself on my damn soul. I stroked her hair, not expecting her to actually speak.

"He's my punishment," she whispered, "if I don't marry you."

Of course. Sergio knew she'd need to be leveraged to be complicit. "Sergio threatened you with Matteo?"

"I told him he couldn't make me speak vows to that man." She fisted a handful of my shirt. "I was given a choice: Act like a true Outfit princess and marry you, or he'd give me to Matteo. As his whore."

My hold on her waist tightened as I pictured all the ways I could kill them both. So many broken bones, so much blood. But it wasn't just them who had done this to her, and for the first time in forever, I felt guilt, true guilt.

"What did Matteo do to you?" I tried hard to keep the edge out of my voice, but it was impossible.

The man had obviously done something to her; otherwise, he wouldn't be Sergio's trump card, and my mind ran wild, my heart pounding out an enraged beat. He looked at her like he thought he owned her, like he could have her….

"It doesn't matter." It did matter, though.

"Emilia…" I hesitated. "Please just tell me, did he…?" Fuck. "Because I swear to God, if he touched you against your will,

I'll send men to kill him right now. I don't give a fuck about your uncle."

"No, he didn't touch me like that," she whispered. "But he would. He's a monster."

Sergio had given her a choice between bad and worse—a man she clearly knew was awful or a man with a reputation for violence. "So you ran because you knew I was a monster, too."

And then I had captured her and offered her that deal. I'd made her believe I would send her back to Chicago, forcing her to pick between the same two fates. I was no better than either of them.

"I thought you were," she said, so quietly I barely heard her.

I stroked over her hair, removing the pins and trailing my fingers through the messy strands. "I am piccola." But I wouldn't be, not to her.

We fell into silence, the soft lull of her breaths the sweetest melody.

I held her all night, woke her when the nightmares racked her body, and soothed her back to sleep. Over and over. I had to wonder just how broken Emilia Donato really was behind that armor and why a nineteen-year-old girl was so guarded. What the fuck had Romano done to her to chase her in sleep like that? I'd find out soon enough. I'd promised Donato that Matteo Romano would survive my city. I hadn't specified in what state.

18

EMILIA

I stood on the sidewalk and glanced up at the industrial-style building in front of me. Lights flashed through barred-over windows, heavy music pulsing from within. Apparently, Gio owned a nightclub, and having seen him at that gala, it made sense. He hid behind a mask of legitimacy.

I inhaled the cool night air, happy to be out of the apartment. I'd basically been trapped in there with Tommy for the last two days. Gio had business to handle, and as much as he loved to personally watch me at all times, apparently, it was too dangerous. I thought I would appreciate the space, but I actually missed his presence, which was concerning. I just slept better with him beside me, that was all. My subconscious was evidently a traitor, right along with my body.

I followed him down a dark side alley that stank of garbage and through the back door into the building. Inside was a dark corridor and a set of stairs that led to an office. It was simple

—a desk, a leather couch, some monitors showing various security camera angles.

The far wall was entirely glass and looked out over the busy nightclub below. I moved closer, watching people dancing and drinking. They looked so free, as though nothing could touch them but the beat of the music, perhaps the sensual touch of a partner. It seemed like a new, forbidden world that I was suddenly eager to taste. It looked like an escape.

Gio's hand landed on my hip, pulling me back against him. He said nothing, but he didn't have to. Ever since I had broken down and cried on him after that meeting with Matteo, I felt like a pane of glass he could see straight through.

It had been two days and I was still grappling to reforge my defenses, but it was hard. I was tired. Tired of fighting a battle it felt like I would never win. Tired of riding the emotional rollercoaster of fear and determination. Seeing my uncle and Matteo had just exacerbated it, reminding me that they'd always be there, stalking my every move, even if I did manage to escape. *If he can't have you, no one can.* I'd never truly be free. And in my moment of weakness, Gio silently offered me a reprieve, a place to rest, even if it was in the arms of a man who should be my enemy. But somewhere along the line, I'd stopped seeing him as that, and in those arms, I found the closest I'd felt to peace in what seemed like a lifetime of war.

Tomorrow, I told myself. Tomorrow I'd fight.

Gio pressed a kiss to the top of my head. I hadn't forgotten our morning in the shower, the way he'd made me come for him with nothing more than dirty words and my own fingers.

The way he'd stroked himself and groaned my name. Yet, he hadn't tried anything since then. Nothing more than sweet kisses that were more reassuring than sexual. He'd let me cry on him... Never mind blurred lines, this felt like a ball of yarn, tangled strands knotting together in a way I couldn't pluck apart. The man could make me hate him, want him, and yearn for the warmth of his embrace all in the same breath. Sex was easy. Sex as a motivation, I understood, but this... whatever was happening right now, it made no sense.

"Why did you bring me here?" I asked.

"Because I have something for you."

"Oh?"

I turned to him, taking in the strain that clung to the angles of his face. I knew he was losing men, that whatever was going on with my uncle and the Irish was escalating. He was a mafia boss, hard and ruthless, but those dead men clearly weighed heavily on him. Yet here he was, offering me gifts.

I opened my mouth to say something, anything. That I was sorry about his men, that I saw what it was costing him— There was a knock on the door that led into the main club, and I tried to pull away from him but had nowhere to go. A pretty blond woman strode inside, the music spiking with her appearance. Her swaying hips faltered when she spotted us, gaze narrowing as she took in Gio pressed up against me. She placed a drink down on his desk, flashing a sultry smile. I instantly hated her for absolutely no reason, which wasn't fair.

"We need to talk," she said, her voice low and raspy, gaze roaming over Gio as he pushed away from me and took a seat behind the desk.

She obviously worked here, and if she hadn't fucked him yet, she wanted to. Why did that bother me so much? He was gorgeous. Of course, she wanted to fuck him. And she was hot, so he'd probably taken her up on it. *There are girls I fuck, and now there is the girl I'll marry.* Was she one of the girls he fucked? I wondered if he made her beg for it, too. It didn't look he'd have to. Did he punish her? Tie her to a bed and spank her?

"Not now, Laylah." He took the drink, barely sparing her a glance.

"It's important, Gio."

Not Giovanni, Gio. A name he'd only insisted I use when he'd made me touch myself for him. Something vicious twisted in my gut, and I swallowed it down.

"Well, then spit it out."

The woman pointedly glanced at me.

"You can discuss business in front of Emilia."

I was pretty sure she didn't want to discuss business.

I wanted to flip her a middle finger. With my left hand. Not like she could miss the massive rock he insisted I wear anytime I left the penthouse. It was stupid. I did not care what Gio did or who he fucked, but evidently, I did because I found myself moving behind his chair. My left hand landed on his shoulder before sliding down his chest… Laylah's gaze burned into mine, and I fought a smirk as anger flared in her pretty hazel eyes.

"It's fine," I said, feigning confidence I did not feel. "I'll go get a drink." I said the words, but some petty yet insecure part of me wanted Gio to stop me, to pick me. Pick me for what, though? Because this entire time, I'd been trying to get him to do anything *but* pick me. God, I needed to stop, walk out of here, and let her fuck him. But I couldn't.

I bent and captured his lips, purely for show, just to drive the point home to this bitch before I left. Before I could pull away, he grasped my jaw, turning the kiss from something chaste to something altogether…not. Teeth scraped over my bottom lip, his tongue seeking mine. My mind instantly clouded until I couldn't focus on anything but his mouth, his touch burning my skin.

"Laylah, get out," he snapped.

I wanted to see the pissed-off look I was sure she'd be wearing right now, but he wouldn't release me, and I couldn't look away from those eyes that seemed like the endless depths of the bluest ocean. Music boomed for a second before the door slammed, blocking it out once more. I started to pull away, but he yanked me forward, forcing me to straddle his thighs.

"Oh, no. You're not escaping after that little display." He clasped the back of my neck, imprisoning me against him.

"What display?"

He chuckled and slid his fingers into my hair, gently pulling my head to the side. "You know exactly what." Warm breath washed over my throat before his lips did. "You're sexy when you're jealous, princess." His lips worked lower, his tongue making occasional swipes that had my skin tingling.

"I'm not jealous."

"So you don't care if I let you go and get that drink while I call Laylah back in here to suck my dick?"

The thought made me irrationally angry, made me want to kick him in the junk and scratch out her eyes. What the hell? That was not okay, and the realization startled me out of whatever lust-fueled trance he had me in.

"I…" I tried to shift off his lap, but he wouldn't let me. "We should—"

"Shhh, it's okay, piccola." He stroked my cheek like I was some panicked wild animal.

"It's not—"

"Yes, it is." He cupped my face in both hands, forcing me to look at him, but I didn't want to.

I didn't want him to witness this…that I cared, that I wanted the man who had bartered for me like a possession to want me and only me, even when I couldn't give him any of myself.

His thumbs swept over my cheeks. "I'd kill any man you'd fucked, on the pure principle that he touched you."

"That's…" Psychopathic? Insane? Weirdly hot? Shit.

"I know, and I don't care. I'm not rational when it comes to you."

I met his unwavering gaze, so certain, so confident. "You've only known me a week, Gio."

"Exactly. I dread to think how volatile I'd be after weeks." He took my hand and kissed the back of it. "Or months." Another kiss. "Years." And another. "Stop trying to make this rational, Emila. It isn't. You're fighting for the sake of fighting."

Was he right? I felt like I was doing battle with myself half the time and only really harming myself in the process. I just couldn't stop…

"I didn't mean to… It's just…" I let out a sigh, focusing on a point over his shoulder just so I didn't have to look at him while I showed a glimmer of weakness. "She looked at you like…" Fuck, I couldn't even say it out loud.

"Like she could have me."

I nodded, and he pressed his lips to mine, coaxing, prying things from me that my body wanted to offer while my mind refused to give up. That kiss said I was his and I was special, and for once in my life, I wanted *to be* special. To someone. To him. I found myself shifting closer until the hard press of him ground between my legs.

"She can't have me." Another kiss. "If any man so much as looked at you the wrong way, piccola, I'd cut his eyes out of his head."

Fuck. I needed to remember why this was a bad idea. *Tomorrow.*

He gripped my hips in both hands, forcing me over him in a way that turned my body liquid. "If anyone thinks he can have you, I'll be sure to remind him exactly who you belong with." *With*, not to—I didn't miss the distinction.

"Gio," I gasped as he thrust up against me. My hips moved of their own volition, chasing that sweet high only he could give. Within seconds I was falling apart, shaking and clinging to him as I rode out the waves of pleasure. And as I came down, all I could think was how amazing it would surely feel to actually fuck him.

He bit my lip, then pushed to his feet and placed me on his desk. His phone vibrated against the wood, and he glanced at the screen with a smile. "This man, for instance…"

A few seconds later, the door clicked open and Philipe shoved another man forward, a gun pointed at his back. A bag covered his head, and I stilled, wondering what the hell was going on. Philipe dragged a chair to the corner of the room before shoving his captive into it, and I noticed the smears of blood on the man's pale-blue shirt. His wrists were cable tied to the arms of the chair, and then Philipe left.

"This man thinks he can have you." There was only one man besides Gio who thought he could have me, who might have pissed off Gio—Matteo Romano. Bleeding and bound and helpless. Gio pulled my gaze back to him. "Can he have you, Emilia?"

"Never."

"And I'll never *let* him have you. Do you trust me?"

"Yes." I was surprised by the truth in that one word.

He stroked my face, the touch soothing and reverent. "He can't see you, but he can hear everything. I'm going to remind him that you belong with me, to me, and he will never have you."

Matteo fought in his restraints, letting out a low growl, and I couldn't help but smile at his helpless state. Was I really going to do this? A little thrill shot through me at the thought. I knew how men like Matteo worked. They coveted purity, to be the first man to touch, to take. No matter what happened,

Matteo would always know that I was tainted by another, that I wanted another. All while he was bound and bloodied, forced to listen to what I would never give him. It wasn't the revenge I craved, but it was something.

I met Gio's gaze and nodded.

"Good girl," he practically purred before kissing me. The kiss was rougher than the last one, possessive, demanding, claiming.

"You are mine, Emilia Donato." He spoke the words like a vow against my lips. My mind fumbled for an argument but came up empty when his teeth sunk into my neck, followed by the warm swipe of his tongue. He pushed me back on the desk, his gaze boring into mine as though waiting for me to stop him when he slid my underwear down my legs.

"Good girl," he whispered when I made no protest, kissing me once more. "I'd never let him see you like this."

I knew he wouldn't. "Are you going to make me come, Gio?" The words sounded foreign on my tongue, like someone else's. I wanted him to, though. I couldn't handle more teasing today.

He groaned, eyes blazing. "Careful. I'll do a lot more than make you come if you say things like that."

He gripped the insides of my thighs, roughly forcing them apart. Cool air washed over sensitive flesh as he stared between my legs. I'd normally feel self-conscious, but I was empowered by his attention.

"Fuck, you look perfect like this, piccola."

I wanted him to touch me so badly—needed it. I wasn't tied up or held down this time; I couldn't pretend that a single thing about this was unwanted. His touch was like a toxin in my blood, pulling me further and further under his spell with every rough stroke, every sharp scrape of his teeth over my throat. My core was throbbing, desperate for something.

He bent and kissed the inside of my thigh, so gently, but it was like a bolt of lightning through my body. "Tell me you're mine, Emilia."

I shook my head and had no warning before his tongue swiped between my legs. "Gio!" Holy shit.

My spine bowed off the desk as heat ripped through me. His tongue circled my clit perfectly, drawing a string of moans from my lips. I wanted all of it, wanted to feel the mindless, toxic pleasure only he could offer. I wanted to slip into the sweet oblivion where nothing could touch me and my shitty reality didn't exist. He was my disease and my cure.

I was writhing on the desk, right on the edge, when he stopped. "Tell me you're *not* mine then, and I'll stop."

Fuck. "No."

He kept going, this time slipping two fingers into my soaked pussy. Shit. He stopped. "Tell me—"

"I fucking hate you," I gasped, and he laughed, hot breath washing over sensitive nerves and making me moan in frustration.

He licked over me again, and my fingers went to his hair, tugging hard as though I could force him to give me what I wanted. He bit the inside of my thigh, the sharp pain cutting through the pleasure building within me.

"Please."

"Say it. Tell me you're mine, Emilia, and I'll lick this sweet cunt and make you scream my name like I'm your own personal god." Fuck, he was so filthy.

"I…"

He placed the softest kiss to my clit, and my entire body trembled with need. "I'm waiting, piccola."

It was just words, words I knew he wanted Matteo to hear. Words I suddenly realized I wanted Matteo to believe because even if I weren't Gio's, I would never be his.

"I'm yours," I breathed.

He hummed against me, making me jerk. "Again."

"I'm yours, Gio." And those words didn't feel like a lie.

He bit my thigh on a groan. "Yes, you fucking are."

Then he buried two fingers deep inside me and ate me like I was his last meal. I fell apart again, screaming his name just like he said I would. I wanted him, hated him, needed him. That orgasm shattered everything that had come before. It tore me apart and pieced me back together with his name engraved on my heart.

The heat of his mouth left me, and I lay on that desk, staring at the ceiling, gasping for breath.

"Fuck, you're beautiful when you come, Emilia."

I was a mess, and he still looked perfect, suit still immaculate. He pulled his fingers out of me, and I immediately missed the feeling. He brought them to my mouth, forcing them past my lips. My gaze held his as I sucked the taste of myself off him, wrapping my tongue around his fingers.

He groaned and closed his eyes. "So perfect. So mine." When he kissed me this time, it was slow and drugging, his tongue brushing over mine, sharing the taste of me between us. "And you put on such a good show for our visitor, princess."

I glanced to where Matteo sat, his body tense. I'd almost forgotten he was here.

"Although you sounded so sweet moaning my name, I'm not sure if I should let him live with that memory." He glared at the poor excuse of a man. "Sergio will probably get pissy if I kill his boy scout."

Gio pulled me to my feet, helping me back into my underwear before tugging my dress down. Then he pressed a kiss to my forehead, lips lingering against my skin as he spoke. "Now, he knows. And if he ever looks at you like he can have you again, I will do as I said and personally deliver his eyeballs to you, my sweet piccola."

And with that gruesome yet oddly romantic image left in my mind, he walked over to Matteo. With the bag on his head, I could almost pretend he was anyone, just some faceless body. But when Gio removed it, sickness rose in the back of my throat. He was the face of my sister's end, the boogeyman I couldn't help but fear. Matteo's angry glare met mine, his teeth gritted around the ball gag in his mouth. Like that, he didn't seem so scary. Gio stepped between us, cutting off his view of me.

"Now you know exactly whose name she's going to be moaning every night."

While the functioning part of my brain got pissed that he would even say that—because, no, I would not be moaning his name every night—the sex-hazed part liked his possession. Maybe it was just because he'd made me come. Twice. Or maybe I just so badly wanted someone to care about me.

"You don't look at her; you don't think her fucking name."

Silence greeted him, of course. Mine and Matteo's.

Gio turned to face me. "I know he did something to you, Emilia." I stilled, and Gio took something from his pocket and handed it to me. A knife. "I find blood quite gratifying for a debt." He stepped aside and swept a hand toward Matteo's bound form.

"Gio, I can't—"

"You can, if you want to." Just like that. If I wanted to.

I stared at the blade in my hand, then at Matteo Romano, a man who featured as the monster in so many of my nightmares and was now helpless. A man who thought nothing of beating my sister over and over again, who had terrified me, now couldn't raise a hand. I gripped the blade, something in me rising up to answer the call of vengeance I didn't even know I needed until that exact moment.

As I approached him, I pictured my sister's tear-stained face as she begged me not to confront Matteo about her black eye that first time because I was only sixteen and it would get me punished. I remembered the way he'd talk to my parents like they were all one big happy family, while my sister lingered behind him, a shadow in her own home. And lastly, I pictured her face in that coffin, how peaceful she had looked in death while the last year of her life had been nothing but brutality.

Matteo had the audacity to glare at me as I stopped in front of him.

"You know, I hate you for what you did to her." I ran my finger over the tip of the blade, the fear I usually felt around him absent. Because he was restrained or because I had a bigger, badder monster at my back. One that was on my side…if I wanted him. If I'd let him.

"You're pathetic. A poor excuse of a man, even by my uncle's low standards." With each passing second, my rage grew, memories that I tried not to think of, that were too painful, now flipping through my mind like a Rolodex. I wanted him dead, but first, he needed to suffer. I didn't want him to look pretty or peaceful in a coffin like she had but as scarred and vile as he really was. My heart thrashed in my chest as I lifted a trembling hand, and he fought his restraints as I pressed the tip of the knife to his temple.

"Careful. You might lose an eye."

A strange sense of calm came over me as I dragged the knife down his cheek. Slowly, so slowly. Blood welled and poured, and the sight of it was like a burning shot of whiskey settling in my stomach or the first sweet mouthful of the most exquisite dessert. Gratifying. Right. Pure satisfaction. His cries were muffled by the gag, but I relished in them. I channeled every inch of pain and suffering and rage into the piece of metal in my hand. He deserved this. Pain and humiliation, to feel weak and powerless. The blood poured over his skin, covering the knife and my hand, soaking into the collar of his shirt. I wanted more. The little demon on my shoulder screamed for it, demanded that it wasn't enough. I moved the blade to his throat, and he stilled, nostrils flaring with rapid breaths. His eyes met mine, burning with fury and something else—fear. Matteo Romano was scared.

"I can see your fear, Matteo. And I'm going to delight in it just as much as you did hers."

He'd made her live in fear, and no one helped her. No one. Not even me. Tears stung my eyes, and I pressed the knife harder against his throat, hand trembling, blood rising beneath the steel. Gio's arm wrapped around my waist, warm breath washing over my neck.

"Stop, piccola," he breathed into my ear.

"He deserves to die." My voice cracked, and I realized tears were tracking down my cheeks.

"But you don't deserve to kill him."

I twisted my head toward Gio, and his free hand stroked over my jaw.

"Death stains you, princess. Even the men who deserve it."

I met his gaze that was so open, so honest, like he'd give me anything I asked for. As if he saw the question in my eyes, he turned me to face him, pulling me away from Matteo.

He brought his lips to my ear. "I made your uncle a promise. For now. If you really want to kill him, I won't stop you. But I promise *you*, I will kill this man for you when this is over. And a vow to you is not one I would ever break." He pulled back and lifted my hand, brushing his lips over my blood-stained knuckles before he plucked the knife from them. "Okay?"

I nodded mutely as reality crashed over me. I was willing to slice open Matteo's throat.

"Philipe!" Gio called, and the man entered the room, shoving the bag over Matteo's head and cutting him loose before dragging him out.

19

GIO

Emilia stood there, staring at the door Romano had just been dragged through. Her hand was still covered in blood, a smudge on her cheek. I wasn't as sick as Jackson, but I had to admit, it did something to me seeing her like this. So savage, so corrupted. In more ways than one.

I had given her that knife because I assumed he'd hurt *her* and I wanted her to take back some power, but now I saw; he hadn't done it to her. Whatever it was, she was ready to kill him for it. I just couldn't let her. After a while, you became numb to death, but I never wanted Emilia to be stained by my world like that.

She folded her arms over her chest, and I could practically see her re-forging her armor. "I'm still not yours," she whispered. "I didn't beg. I just said it for…him." One step forward and two back, all the damn time, as if any glimmer of surrender had to be combated on pure principle. Something had just happened between us, a shift, and I wasn't about to let her deny it.

My temper rose, and I gripped her throat. "You can fight and hiss and scratch all you like, Emilia, but deep down, you want to be mine." I tugged her close and dragged my nose up the side of her throat, inhaling the scent of her. "Because you know I'll fuck you and look after you." I pressed a kiss to her jaw. "And if anyone hurts you—past, present, or future—I'll kill for you."

Emilia Donato was a wolf in sheep's clothing. Given the chance, she could be fierce, but beneath all her fight, she wanted this. For someone to fight *for* her. Because I could tell no one ever had.

"Now, are you going to tell me what he did to make you hate him enough to kill?"

A slow nod. I took her hand, guiding her to the couch. The music from the club still rumbled around us, but it did nothing to cut through the tension radiating from Emilia's stiff shoulders.

I pulled her into my lap, and she didn't argue. "Who did he hurt?"

She looked away from me, eyes glazing as she focused on a spot on the wall. "My sister."

I took her hand in my own, the blood now drying and sticky. "Tell me about her." This felt pivotal somehow.

Emilia was so open in many ways, so easy to read, but there was a whole side of her she kept locked down, and I wanted it. I wanted to know every detail of her life. Her pain, her pleasure, what made her cry or smile. For long moments she remained silent, and I expected her to shut me out.

"Chiara was the good one, the dutiful daughter. She was kind and sweet and so naïve," Emilia choked. "She believed the bullshit my parents fed her, that women in The Outfit were protected and cherished. Thought she'd get married to someone they picked just for her and live this happy life…" she trailed off, eyes closing as her brows pinched together. "Uncle Sergio gave her to him like a broodmare he no longer wanted. Matteo abused her, beat her, raped her." Her voice broke, and I held her tighter, as though I could physically keep my little kitten together. She came to me, burying her face in my throat, and it felt like the sweetest gift—her vulnerability, her trust.

"When she got pregnant, she knew she'd be trapped forever." Small fingers fisted in my shirt. "She killed herself." Her voice was barely above a whisper, her pain a raw wound that I felt as if it were my own.

And just like that, it all made sense. For the first time, I saw Emilia clearly. The armor she wore was forged in suffering, her mistrust warranted, because her family had sold her sister, and given the opportunity, they had done exactly the same thing to her, giving her to me. And when she didn't want it, they had threatened to give her to the very same creature who had driven her sister to her grave. No wonder Emilia feared him. No wonder she had run. Why would she trust anyone? Except for maybe Renzo Donato.

"I'm sorry, piccola."

She felt so small and fragile in my arms, and fuck if I didn't want to slaughter everyone who had ever hurt her. But I was one of them.

My phone rang, and I took it from my pocket, sending Jackson to voicemail. I wanted to tell Emilia that I released her from our agreement, from whatever this was, but I couldn't bring myself to say the words. It was selfish, but I couldn't let her go, and I knew the second I did, she'd run and wouldn't look back.

Instead, I stroked her cheek. "Say the word, Emilia, and I'll kill everyone who played any part in Chiara's death."

She closed her eyes, leaning into my touch as tears clung to her lashes. So beautifully broken, my fragile little kitten.

Jackson rang again, and I let out a frustrated growl.

She swiped at the tears on her face. "Answer it."

I clamped a hand on her hip before she could escape and answered the phone. "What?"

"Tommy's been shot."

My whole world came to a grinding halt, my heart hitting my damn throat. "What?"

"Irish hit. He's in the hospital. I…" Jackson's voice broke. "I don't think he's gonna make it, Gio."

I hated hospitals. Death seemed to linger in the air, not even offering its victims the dignity of speed. Emilia and Jackson sat in the corner of the busy waiting room, my enforcer still covered in blood—Tommy's blood. Too much for me to believe he could possibly pull through this. Three bullets to the chest. I paced across the waiting room, my stomach knotting. Fuck, if he died… he was my friend, my brother, my family.

"Gio—" Jackson started.

I held up my hand, silencing him. I didn't want to hear what he had to say right now.

The double doors that led to the hospital rooms opened, and Una and Nero stepped through them.

Nero clapped a hand on my shoulder. "He pulled through the surgery, but they're keeping him in a coma for the next two days. We just have to wait…." His brows were pulled together, and I knew he was struggling as much as I was to process this.

We were supposed to be untouchable. Had been for years. No one dared to come for us, and I knew from the look on his face that Nero was about to remind every-fucking-body why.

Una approached Jackson and whispered something into his ear.

He nodded and stood. "We're going to find this fucker," he announced.

I nodded, unable to even give orders. Maybe I shouldn't be giving them. I'd gotten us into this. Gotten Tommy into this. Nero was feared enough to keep everyone away from us. I tried to be better than the bloodshed and violence and constant war, but better wasn't what kept my family safe.

Jackson walked out with Una.

Nero glanced from me to Emilia sitting silently behind me. "You can go see him. Want me to stay with her?"

"No, it's okay." I held out my hand to Emilia, and she pushed to her feet, threading her fingers through mine.

I wasn't prepared when we stepped into Tommy's hospital room. I'd seen countless men die, ended them myself, maimed and tortured. This was different. The lack of violence was what made it disturbing. The silence permeated only by the click and rasp of the ventilator breathing for him. It hurt to see him so helpless. It hurt to *be* so helpless. The tubes and wires all served as a reminder of just how fragile he was right now, how tentatively he clung to life.

Emilia took a step toward him, tears shining on her cheeks. She didn't know him like I did, but she'd spent time with him. And like anyone who spent more than five minutes in Tommy's presence, she liked him.

"I can wait in the waiting room," she said quietly. "I won't run. I promise."

Did I want her to go? No. I'd always weathered my grievances alone, violence and whiskey my own brand of therapy. But here she was, like some angel, offering me a dose of reprieve in my suffering.

"No. Stay."

With a small nod, she took a seat on the far side of the bed, taking Tommy's limp hand in hers. When I sat beside her, she took mine, too, acting as a link between us. And that was how we remained for hours, a silent vigil in that hospital room. If he had any awareness, I wanted him to know I was here. That I would be there for him where I had failed before. Guilt was like a damn knife in my chest, twisting with each passing minute until I was full of self-loathing. If he died... No, he would not die.

The nurses finally kicked us out at midnight, and it wasn't until the early hours of the morning, when I held Emilia in the darkness, that she finally spoke.

"It's not your fault, Gio."

It was, though. I was the boss, and that meant every single decision that led to this point was on me. I should have known that kid was Shane O'Hara long before he had ended up dead. I'd dropped the ball. Because I was distracted at a time when I should have been one hundred percent focused.

Emilia rolled over and placed her palm on my cheek. "He'll pull through. He's too stubborn and annoyingly optimistic to die."

I hoped she was right because I didn't know what I'd do without him.

———

I pulled up outside the warehouse on the outskirts of Queens. Emilia sat in the passenger seat, her gaze shifting around the series of dilapidated and shadowy buildings. I should have left her at the hospital with Tommy. I didn't really know why I'd brought her. All day, my mind had been a rollercoaster of blame and repeated conversations, memories… things I could have done differently. Emilia being one of them.

So, maybe some fucked up bit of me wanted her to see this and for her to run because I told myself that this time I might just let her go. That I needed to because my obsession with her was bad for us both. But what I should do and would do were—as always with her—conflicted.

"Stay here."

I got out of the car and walked toward the warehouse. The last twenty-four hours had been a blur of whiskey and rage, and this was the culmination of that because Una had found the guy who had shot Tommy, and I was about to unleash the kind of retribution I rarely allowed on this man. That feral bloodlust pulsed through my veins like poison. I wanted to maim, kill, and destroy anyone and everyone who played a single part in harming Tommy. A couple of cars were parked inside the dilapidated building, their headlights illuminating the gruesome scene before me.

The place was long abandoned, but in the center was a single man, David O'Hara, his bound wrists hooked to a chain in the ceiling. He was beaten and bloody, cuts littering his bare torso, both eyes swollen shut. One nipple was missing, a stream of blood running from the spot like a tap. The place was a symphony of Jackson's fists hitting his flesh over and over again, the ominous creak of the chain and a slow, drip, drip, drip of blood spattering the dusty concrete. Shadows swayed back and forth in the headlights along with his body, like demons dancing and writhing on the walls.

A few of Jackson's men lingered nearby, none daring to get too close. Probably because Una sat on the hood of the nearby SUV, flipping a knife in her hand. Tommy was one of the few people she cared about. When Jackson stepped back, she took his place, a cold smile on her face as she placed the knife to his chest and dug the blade in. He screamed and bucked as she cut off his other nipple.

"Please," he begged.

I smiled. "You'll find no mercy here, but you're welcome to beg for your worthless life."

Tommy hadn't even been given that chance.

Una started carving lines into his flesh, turning him into her own personal canvas. She wasn't usually so gratuitous. Violence always had a purpose with her, and I was the same, but this was different. This wasn't logical and calculated because this man tried to take someone from us. The fact was, Tommy should be dead right now, and he was hanging on by a thread. Thanks to this piece of shit.

"Jackson." I glanced at my friend, and he flashed me a vicious grin.

"Want me to deprive him of a few fingers?"

I nodded. "Shoot him up first. He looks like he's on the verge of passing out."

Jackson pulled a case from the trunk of the car and drew up a syringe of adrenaline. The second he jabbed it into the side of David's neck, he jerked, thrashing like a fish on a line. Jackson laughed. "And welcome back to your own personal hell. Fingers or toes?"

"Fingers." Una wrinkled her nose. "Feet are disgusting."

For the next half an hour, the pair of them picked O'Hara apart, piece by piece, filling him with adrenaline every time he got too close to the edge. But he was dying. His blood pooled over the floor beneath him like a morbid mirror, reflecting the lights and a grizzly version of an already ugly scene.

"Enough," I said when Jackson removed his last finger.

His hands were now stumps, the blood running down his arms and over his chest like some morbid fountain. His head hung limply, legs buckling. I gripped his chin and slapped his cheek, forcing him to look at me through half-closed eyes.

"You killed my son," he gasped, the words muffled by his swollen lips and undoubtedly broken jaw.

He was right. We'd killed his son, and he'd tried to kill Tommy, and if I were logical right now, I'd try to stop the cycle of blood, but I wasn't logical. He'd tried to kill Tommy, and I didn't give a fuck what had led to that. This man would pay for his grave misjudgment of coming after me and mine.

"I did, and now I'm going to kill you." I held out my hand, and Jackson placed a knife in it. I'd usually shoot him, but I wanted to look him in the eye and see the very moment when his worthless life left him. I placed the blade to his throat.

There was no fear in his eyes, only acceptance. He had to have known this would be his end the moment he pulled that trigger, but the drive for revenge regardless of consequence… well, that was something I understood right then.

I dragged the blade across his neck, opening his throat from ear to ear. It gushed, spattering the concrete as he choked. And I looked him in the eye, watching his life dull and fade to nothing. Until he simply ceased to exist.

"Send him to Patrick O'Hara."

When I turned around, Emilia was standing in the doorway of the warehouse, slim arms folded over her chest, brow furrowed. I could barely look at her as I approached. She already thought I was a monster, but the truth was, she had no idea what I was capable of. This was the tip of the iceberg.

"Get in the car."

20

EMILIA

I couldn't sleep. My mind was full of nightmares waiting to creep up on me the second I closed my eyes. Tommy in that hospital bed, holding onto life, just like Chiara had, after... He was kind and good, just like her. Why did horrible things always seem to happen to the best people? Meanwhile, men like Sergio and Matteo seemed to just survive, despite their chosen profession. It wasn't fair.

The moment we arrived back, Gio had left me and gone to meet my uncle at his hotel. They were on the war path, it seemed.

He said nothing about what happened in that warehouse, and I knew Gio hadn't wanted me to see that—the violence, the blood. It didn't bother me like I thought it would, like it probably should have. There was a certain beauty in his retribution, a morbid form of justice. Tommy deserved justice, and Gio had delivered it for him. Just like that. Because he had the power, with a click of his fingers, he could make someone pay and end their life. And in the face of such brutal violence, all I could think was that no one had ever done that for Chiara. There was no Gio to avenge her. Maybe he'd keep his word. Maybe one day he would kill Matteo for me, for her.

I glanced at the spot where he should be, and a horrible empty feeling settled in my gut. He was hurting, grieving for his friend, and I wanted to help him. I just didn't know how. I'd been where he was, but my story didn't have a happy ending, no glimmer of hope I could offer him. I found myself wanting to shoulder his grief nonetheless because though he may not have known he was doing it, over the last few days, he'd shouldered plenty of mine.

I got out of bed and padded down the hall before stopping in the open doorway of his office. He sat behind his desk, back to me and whiskey glass in hand as he stared out over the glittering lights of the city.

The floorboard creaked under my foot, and he turned to me, his gaze even cooler than usual. Moonlight spilled around him, washing him in tones of silver. He looked so untouchable, a cold king on a throne, lording over his city. Like this, he intimidated me, scared me even, and I had the urge to turn around and run away. I knew that was what he wanted, though, to scare me off, so he could suffer and wallow in his own despair. He blamed himself for Tommy, but I'd also seen the look on his face after he cut that man's throat. He hid it well, but he was ashamed. That he'd done it, or just that I'd seen it, I wasn't sure.

Stealing myself, I stepped into the room and approached him. He didn't move a muscle, and my heart thrummed an anxious beat as I forced myself to crawl into his lap and wrap my arms around his neck. There was a single tense moment where I thought he might reject me, but then he cracked, arms slowly coming around me, his chin resting on top of my head. A staggered breath rattled his chest, and for long minutes, we just stayed like that. I took comfort in him as much as he did me. Sometimes we felt like two broken halves of the whole, and the only time I felt truly together was here, in his arms, whole.

"I'm sorry, Gio." I squeezed tighter. "I'm sorry your friend is hurt."

"We need to talk," he murmured, and I instantly felt sick because those words sounded so ominous.

I knew I didn't want to hear what he had to say, knew what was coming. Panic fluttered in my chest like the rapid beat of a hummingbird's wings.

I grabbed his face, pressing my lips to his. Kissing him felt so right, like coming home when I'd never really belonged before. That kiss was a silent plea, and I wanted him to hear the words I couldn't bring myself to say. His fingers threaded through my hair, holding me to him as if I were his lifeline, as if he would never let go.

I rested my forehead against his, nails scratching over his stubble.

"I fucked up." He inhaled a deep breath and closed his eyes. "I can't do this anymore."

My heart dropped, or maybe it was cracking. I pulled away from him enough to take in the resolute expression on his face.

"I'm distracted. This was supposed to be a simple marriage arrangement." He was sending me back to Chicago.

I pushed off him, needing distance between us as I absorbed his words. He was giving up. Wait, wasn't that what I'd wanted this whole time?

"Tommy never should have been in a position to get shot. That's on me." And me, apparently.

"You blame me?"

He swiped a hand over his tired face. "No, Emilia, I blame me."

"You're going to hand me back to my uncle?" My voice cracked, betraying the horror that was starting to wind around my throat like the fingers of death. Oh my God, he was going to give me to Matteo. After what I had done in that club… he'd kill me for sure. I couldn't breathe.

Gio pushed to his feet and reached for me, but I backed away. "Emilia, calm down. Of course not. I've arranged for you to stay in one of my apartments—"

"You said I was yours." The words were weak and thready, and though I'd fought them, him going back on them hurt.

"You don't want this!" he roared. "And I want you too much. It drives me mad, chasing what I can't fucking have." He dragged an agitated hand through his hair. "You distract me, Emilia, and it might have cost Tommy his life."

I'd hated him and fought him and done everything to avoid marrying him. But now, when he finally gave up, when he was willing to let me go, I realized it was the last thing I wanted.

"You are still mine, though. No one will hurt—"

I closed the distance between us and placed my fingers over his lips. "You're right. I don't want to marry you. I don't want your deals, or for you to coerce me, or threaten me, or buy me…." I dropped my hand and met his gaze, fighting tears. "I won't beg you to marry me, just so I can live. I won't marry you just so I don't get handed off to Matteo Romano as a whore." My voice hitched, and he cupped my cheek, calloused thumb sweeping over my jaw. "But I can't pretend anymore that I don't *want* you."

He stilled.

"Just you. And me. And this." I placed my hand on his chest, sliding my palm over the material of his shirt. I wanted him. I wanted him to allow me a single moment without all the strings that came with being his. I wanted him to be the first man I willingly gave myself to while I still could.

"It's more complicated than that," he whispered.

I shook my head. "*This* isn't complicated. So give me this. For one night. No begging, no deals…."

His eyes searched mine as an agonizing moment passed between us. Then he kissed me. He kissed me like a man searching for the meaning of his very existence, and I kissed him back like I wanted to be it. His hands went to my waist, my thighs wrapping around him as he carried me to his bedroom.

"I'm not going to make you beg, piccola." He lowered me to my feet at the end of his bed and grabbed the hem of my shirt, slowly sliding it up my body. Rough fingers grazed over my skin, inch by torturous inch, as his lips brushed my ear. "But you will submit like the good little girl I know you are."

The way he said it had me panting, longing for the battle of wills we always had.

I lifted my arms, and he slid the shirt over my head, stepping back to take in my naked body.

"Fuck."

I had the urge to cover myself, but the look in his eyes made me pause. He fisted my hair before his lips crashed over mine, hard and angry and barely restrained.

"Get on your knees, princess," he commanded against my lips.

I hesitated, unable to simply bow to him. We both knew I would eventually, but I liked the struggle before we got there.

He smiled like the devil himself. "Strike one."

The thought of him spanking me again had heat flushing my skin, but I'd sooner kneel than admit I secretly liked his palm on my ass. Conflicted. He always left me conflicted, mind warring with my body. I reluctantly dropped to my knees. His fingers never loosened from my hair, and I knew he loved this—the power, the domination. It was ingrained in him, a fundamental part of who he was. It was what made people fear him, but as I glanced up at him, his expression tinging on feral, I realized I held more power over Giovanni Guerra in this moment than maybe anyone ever had. And I wanted more, everything he had to give. With a trembling hand, I reached for his belt and released it. His fingers flinched in my hair at the sound of his zipper lowering. I only tore my gaze from his face when his dick sprung free, hard and angry looking. I traced one finger over the velvety skin, and he groaned as though I'd grabbed it.

"Fuck, you look so perfect on your knees for me." His hips thrust forward slightly as though he couldn't help himself. "Lick it, princess. Taste what you do to me."

Grabbing his cock, I leaned forward and swiped my tongue over the head, tasting the little bead of salty liquid that had gathered there.

"Fuck." The word was a drawn-out groan that had every muscle in Gio's body tensing.

Oh, yeah. This was how you brought a powerful man to his knees, even if I was the one quite literally on mine. When I took him into my mouth the way I'd seen in pornos, he lost it, thrusting forward until he hit my gag reflex and I wretched.

"Breathe through your nose and swallow, Emilia."

I did, and he groaned, again and again. And when he was absolutely wild, he released me, pulling out of my mouth and dragging both hands through his hair. "Fuck, you're a goddamn problem, princess."

I pushed to my feet, my confidence bolstered by how undone he seemed. Reaching for his shirt, I popped a button, then another. "Did I do a good job?"

He huffed a small laugh, his smile truly devastating as his knuckles brushed my cheek. "Such a good job. You're such a good girl."

I hated that I liked those words so much. They should have been condescending, but my entire body melted at them, the urge to please him like an itch I couldn't quite satisfy.

"Do you like making me lose my mind for you?" He trailed his hand down my throat, over my sensitive breasts and the length of my stomach. By the time he reached between my thighs, I was ready to rub myself all over him. His gaze held mine as he dragged one finger over me, teasing.

I wanted more. So much more.

"This dripping pussy says you like sucking my cock." The words were a breathy groan. His free hand slipped to the back of my neck, his thumb working soothing circles over my skin before he thrust two fingers into me hard enough to push me on tiptoes. I could hear how wet I was, but I couldn't find it in me to be embarrassed.

I wanted this. For myself. Because even if the mafia were never involved and I was just a normal girl, I would want Giovanni Guerra. And I wanted him to have the one thing my father and uncle had tried so hard to preserve. I'd never had a choice over anything in my life apart from this exact moment, and I chose him. He was the key to my shackles, and it occurred to me that while I'd been trying to escape him to find freedom, perhaps he was that freedom.

With careful strokes, he teased an orgasm from me, then slipped his fingers into his mouth, sucking the taste of me from them like it was a delicacy he couldn't get enough of. My pussy clenched at the sight, my blood heating.

"Fuck me, Gio."

It was like a red rag to a bull. His fists clenched, the only sign that he even attempted to show restraint before he moved. His hands went to my waist before he tossed me onto the bed. I expected him to follow, but instead, he stopped, staring down at me.

"Be sure you want this, piccola." His gaze raked over me, a tortured edge to it. "I can't be gentle. And you can't take it back—"

"Gio." This might have been the *only* thing I'd ever been sure of, but I loved that he wanted it to be my choice. I spread my legs, and his gaze dropped to my pussy, eyes flashing as his jaw ticced. "I want you."

His restraint snapped, and he shed his clothes in record time. When he crawled over me, I slid my palms over his warm chest, tracing the lines of ink over hard muscle the way I'd always wanted to. I brushed the line of stitches at his ribs, knowing he'd wear my mark long after I was gone, just as surely as I'd wear the ones he had left on my skin and heart.

His mouth slammed over mine, teeth sinking into my bottom lip as one hand gripped my hip, yanking me toward him. And then he was right there, his dick pressing against me. My stomach clenched nervously, muscles tensing as I waited.

"I have imagined you like this so many fucking times." He moved over me, his cock sliding against me, over me, sending sparks of electricity skittering through my body. "Wet, willing."

My nails dug into his back, and the nerves retreated, replaced by want. He thrust against me again, and I threw my head back on a moan. Fuck.

"That's it, princess. Relax."

I felt the nudge of him at my entrance. He kissed me and then pushed forward in one powerful thrust. The pain had a choked breath slipping past my lips. I didn't know what I had thought losing my virginity would be like, but it wasn't that.

21

GIO

Emilia went rigid beneath me, short nails digging into my chest as though she was trying to cling to me. I couldn't think, couldn't move, because my dick was in a vise grip of tight, warm pussy. I'd never taken anyone's virginity before, and it was a special brand of torture because all I wanted to do was move. But I couldn't. I wouldn't hurt her any more than I already was.

"I'm sorry." I kissed her. "You take me so well. Such a good girl. Just breathe, Emilia."

"I just… need a minute," she whispered.

Fuck. Her pain was like a punch to the gut. Sitting up, I glanced down as I pulled out of her perfect little pussy. My dick was streaked in red, and I groaned at the sight.

"Your blood looks so good on my cock, princess." A feral kind of need gripped me at the sight of it.

That blood was mine. *She* was mine. No one else had ever been inside her, and they never fucking would. I wanted every bit of that sweet gift she'd just given me. I gripped my cock, stroking over it, smearing her that crimson streak and moisture over the length. Fuck. I stared at her pussy as I did, wanting to taste her again, to sample her ruined innocence.

My shoulders forced her thighs apart before I dragged my tongue over the length of her slit. The sweet taste of her mixed with the metallic tang had my dick throbbing, and I released it before I came all over the sheets like a sixteen-year-old boy.

"Fuck, Gio." Her fingers went to my hair, pulling and tugging. She moaned as I thrust my tongue inside her, then circled her clit, over and over until she was writhing on the bed, incoherent words falling from her lips.

I'd fucked countless women, all of whom knew what they were doing, and yet, virginal little Emilia Donato was sending me over the edge. I felt feral, out of control. Rabid.

"I want you screaming my name." I thrust my tongue inside her again, loving the way her greedy little pussy clenched and pulsed in response. "Come for me, Emila. All over my tongue."

Within seconds she was screaming my name like I was her own personal god, and I couldn't take anymore. I needed her more than air in my lungs right then. She was still trembling and panting when I gripped her thighs and wrenched her down the bed. When I thrust inside her, I let out a groan. Nothing had ever felt so right. A man like me shouldn't have a weakness, but I didn't even care. I wanted to be weak for her.

"So perfect. So mine." I kissed her, and her tongue met mine, so eager, so open.

This time when I moved, her hips rolled against me, inviting me in. She felt like a taste of the heaven I knew I would never reach, and I wanted to embrace every earthly moment of it.

"Never fucking letting you go, Emila."

She scratched her nails over my stubble as he lips lingered against mine. "I choose you, Gio. No matter what happens next."

What happened next was I married her and buried my dick in her like this as many times as I possibly could.

I gripped her throat, my tattooed fingers so tainted against her flawless skin. "Mine." I moved over her, and her breathy little gasps were the sweetest music to my ears.

She felt too good, though. Her tight pussy, the exposed emotion in her eyes, the taste of her blood on my tongue... I came hard, my entire body locking down as wave after wave of sheer ecstasy ripped through me. In a single moment, Emilia Donato raked her nails in deep—literally and figuratively—and I wanted her to engrave her name on my damn soul.

"Fuck, Emilia," I groaned before collapsing on top of her. "Such a good girl."

When I could breathe and walk, I went to the bathroom and got a washcloth. She looked like a goddess spread out on my bed, naked, eyes bright, hair wild. My come was smeared on her thighs, dripping from her abused pussy. Fuck. My dick twitched again, and I swear to God, I was going to spend the next week fucking her. When I moved to press the cloth between her legs, she blushed and tried to close them.

I smirked. "Really?"

"It's…I can take care of myself." How I hated those damn words.

"But you're not going to." I lifted a brow when she opened her mouth to argue. "I'm just waiting on that strike two, Emilia. I won't fuck you again tonight, but don't think I won't spank you."

She fell into silence, and I smiled.

"Now…" I threw the washcloth into the hamper before getting her some painkillers and water. "Take those and drink the water."

The defiance was written all over her, but my guess was that she was sore and didn't feel like a spanking tonight. So, she did as she was told.

"Good girl."

I turned out the light and got into the bed beside her. Emilia was guarded and challenging most of the time, but at night, in my bed, she was different. As though here, on this square of foam, the battle lines between us no longer existed. But tonight, she rolled away from me, trying to force space between us. Like fuck was she finally admitting she wanted me, giving herself to me, only to throw a wall between us now. I dragged her against me, realizing my error too late. Her naked body against mine was sheer hell but worth it. After a few seconds, her fingers threaded through mine against her chest, and she held on like I was her damn lifeline. And I would be. Always.

Emilia was a shaft of pure, blinding light in my dark world, and I basked in her warmth. Sometimes she blazed red hot and burned me, but I indulged in the pain, too. I hadn't even realized how cold my life was before her.

I was going to end the mob, and then I was going to marry Emilia Donato. She'd all but sealed our fate with her virgin blood.

———

I woke to the sound of my phone ringing, the flashing screen lighting up the room. The clock on the nightstand read two in the morning. Who the hell was calling me at this time? My heart hiccupped at the sight of Jackson's name on the screen. Tommy.

I climbed out of bed, not wanting to wake up Emilia, but when I glanced at her spot, it was empty. With a frown, I answered the phone. "Yeah."

"Where the fuck have you been?" he snapped.

"Is Tommy okay?"

"What? Yeah. I think so."

I released a sigh of relief. "Okay. Good. Why the fuck are you calling me at two in the morning then?"

"Well, if you looked, you'd see you have ten missed calls." There was the sound of other voices in the background and screaming. "We found the rat."

My grip on the phone tightened. "Who?"

"It was Andreas." That piece of shit motherfucker. Our world was dark and sordid enough, but the one thing we thought we could rely on was loyalty, that the guys in the trenches with us had our backs. Without that….well, we had nothing.

I went to the window, pressing my forehead to the cool glass. "How did you find him?" We'd been looking for weeks, and the bastard had covered his tracks well.

"I had a meeting with some of my capos last night. Renzo Donato recognized him. Says he's seen him at one of Sergio's bars before."

"Wait." It felt like my own heartbeat fucking stilled with those words. "Sergio?"

"He's not a rat for the mob, Gio. He's a rat for Sergio Donato."

My whole world stopped spinning for a moment as the full gravity of that information hit me. "You're sure? The mob isn't setting us up?"

"Between what Renzo said and the information I extracted from Andreas… pretty fucking sure."

Renzo had no reason to lie. From what I could tell, he was loyal to his sister and had no love for Sergio.

"Sergio has been feeding the mob information from his source. He orchestrated all of this bullshit."

I ran through every interaction I'd had with Sergio since the beginning of this so-called alliance. He'd set me up. Which meant… "She was in on it," I breathed, my heart thumping heavily in my chest, something cracking inside me.

"Gio, you don't know—"

"I have to go. Keep me updated." I hung up before he could respond and stormed through the penthouse, looking for Emilia.

I made it to the living room before my phone rang again—Philipe. I fucking knew what he was going to say before I even answered it. "What?" I barked.

"Sir, Miss Donato escaped."

I pinched the bridge of my nose, trying to grapple with the two sides of myself. The boss who needed to protect his interests and his family, and the guy who just got fucked over by a woman he was starting to— No. I shut down the thought.

"She...I removed my men from the hallway like you asked." Because she was with me, safe, and I had stupidly trusted her. "I was in the parking garage." There was a long pause. "She had a gun, and she shot me in the leg. I'm sorry. You told me not to hurt her, and I couldn't follow... But Adamo is following her and awaiting your orders. I'm sorry." He was rambling, stumbling over his words, but I was striding back to my room.

When I opened the nightstand, my gun was gone. She knew how to use a gun...

She'd been working with Sergio this entire time. Played the broken, fighting little damsel with a dead sister... "Tell Adamo I want her unharmed and returned to me." Because I would be the one to hurt her. Maybe I really would tie her to my bed like a pet this time.

I was angry beyond reason but worse, I was hurt, and men like me didn't get hurt. Men like me were supposed to be invulnerable, and maybe that was her entire purpose. Emilia Donato was a trojan horse designed to rip me apart from the inside. And she might have succeeded.

22

EMILIA

I lay there in the darkness, Gio's even breaths a melody I would have listened to forever if I could. I always knew he would have to call time on our weird limbo eventually. I never meant to distract him or for it to result in anyone getting hurt. He wanted marriage, and honestly, I wanted to give in, to be with him, because Giovanni Guerra was a man I could love. But it was exactly what my father and Uncle Sergio wanted me to do. Rolling over for them felt like an acceptance of what they had done to me, to Chiara. It would make me complicit in everything they did to her, the marriage, the abuse, her death. I just couldn't.

And he couldn't keep doing this dance with me while he had an empire to run and a war to fight. We had our one night, and I knew he wanted to send me off to some apartment, but he wouldn't just keep me safe forever. I didn't want him to. I wanted to be free. Of him, of my family, of this pain and grief that hung over me like a dark cloud, tainting everything. But I'd never be free of The Outfit or the brutal injustice of Chiara's death. Not while Matteo and Sergio lived.

The only way I would ever truly find peace was with them both dead. Would Gio kill Sergio and Matteo for me if I asked him to? Maybe. Or maybe I didn't need him to…. Sergio was in New York. And he'd be in the same hotel he always stayed in, the same suite…. The thought teased the edges of my mind, calling to me, demanding I answer a higher power, something greater than myself. No one could get closer to him than me. They thought I was the girl they broke, but I would be the weapon they had forged.

That was how I found myself outside the Forsyth Hotel, the weight of Gio's gun pressing into my back as I stared at the shiny exterior.

Escaping was easier than I thought it would be. The key card to the front door was in his jacket pocket, the same as always, his gun in the nightstand. It was easy, really, easy enough that I could have done it on any of the nights that I'd slept in his bed and had access to his room. But I hadn't because I wasn't sure I truly wanted to escape him anymore. Because I felt safer with him than out here in the big wide world.

I'd been so grateful to find none of his men in the hall because I didn't want to hurt anyone. Until I had to. I felt bad for shooting Philipe, but given what I was about to do, I could afford no room for weak sentiment.

Pushing those thoughts away, I stepped into the hotel's lobby, taking in the marble floors and glittering chandeliers. An older man I recognized as one of my father's capos approached when he spotted me.

His brows were pulled together in a tight frown. "Emilia Donato. You should not be here."

"I need to see my uncle."

"He's not—"

"Take me to him, or I'll be sure to inform him that he missed out on valuable information because of you, Julius." It was bullshit. I had nothing to say to Sergio.

Julius's brows rose as though he was surprised I knew who he was, or perhaps he just didn't expect me to talk to him like that. He didn't even pat me down before escorting me to the elevator. After all, I was just a woman. Weak. Subservient.

When the doors opened on the top floor, I was led to my uncle's suite. With every muted step over the thick carpet, my heartbeat threatened to choke me. This was it. Vengeance for my sister had never seemed like a possibility, but the moment I'd decided on this path, it felt like my sole purpose. I'd never thought I could bring myself to kill my own uncle before, but my time with Gio and Tommy had shown me that family was not blood. It was loyalty and love. I had no love or loyalty for Sergio.

If I succeeded, then killing the boss of the Chicago Outfit would have consequences. My only hope was that the ring on my finger would buy me some time. There wasn't a man in The Outfit who didn't fear the name Giovanni Guerra, and I was sure none of them wanted to be the one to kill his fiancee. They weren't to know it was all fake.

Two men stood outside my uncle's suite, and both ignored me as Julius knocked on the door. I held my breath, pulse-pounding against my eardrums as I waited. I couldn't just shoot him if I wanted to survive, and despite knowing the odds weren't great either way, I wasn't suicidal. I needed to be inside, away from his men and their guns.

When the door finally opened, I stilled, a mix of horror and disappointment punching me in the chest. It wasn't Sergio. My father stood in the doorway, a frown marring his face as he took me in.

"Emilia?" Then his eyes widened. "What are you doing here?" His gaze shifted behind me before he grabbed my arm and dragged me inside, slamming the door behind us.

For a moment, I thought he might be worried about my uncle finding me here or Gio.

"Is Uncle Sergio here?"

He frowned. "No. Why do you want to see him?" When I didn't answer, he squeezed my arm tighter. "Did you run away?"

"Yes." Kind of.

He shook his head, a frown cutting across his aging features. "You have to go back."

I tried to smother the jab of pain in my chest, the crippling disappointment that I should have known to expect whenever my father was concerned. "Aren't you even going to ask me why I ran?"

He paced in front of me, raking a hand through his graying hair. "You can't be here. We cannot afford any dissension between Guerra and us right now." He stopped and half pushed me back toward the door. "If he thinks I helped you—"

I pulled away from him, the hurt worsening as though he were literally twisting a knife in my heart. "What? He might think you're a loving father? What a lie that would be."

He glared at me. "That's not—"

"Not true? Oh, but it is." That blade burrowed deeper with each passing second. "Do you even care if he hurts me or rapes me?"

The words felt like ash in my mouth because Gio would never do either, but he could have. He could have been every bit as bad as Matteo, and my own father would happily send me back to him, as long as his precious alliance held up.

He stepped toward me. "Emilia, I love you."

I backed away, an eery cold settling over me even as rage permeated every inch of my being. "Is that what you said to Chiara? That you loved her?" I shoved him in the chest, wanting a reaction from a man who had never done anything of note in his worthless life. "Did she come to you like this? Did she ask for help, only for you to send her right back to the very fucking monster who hurt her and raped her, over and over?" My voice was rising and breaking at the same time. I shoved him again, harder this time.

He stumbled slightly and folded his arms over his chest, his bulk straining against his suit jacket. "Your sister was ill."

"She wasn't fucking ill! She needed your help."

He'd shown time and time again that he didn't care, but I guess I always hoped that one day he would stand up to my uncle. If not for me, then for her.

"You were her father." I sucked in a sharp breath. "You're *my* father."

"You need to go back to Guerra, Emilia." His expression shuttered, and my heart broke. "You'll either be dragged back to him or sent to Matteo. You know those are your only options."

Yes, because he would never fight for me, the same way he hadn't fought for Chiara.

"You might as well have killed her," I whispered, more to myself than him.

He did nothing. He would always *do nothing.*

A strange sense of peace washed over me, an acceptance of sorts. I could not control other people's actions, only my own. I could not make this man better than he was, only pass judgment on his failings. It was like all my emotions just switched off as I realized what I had to do.

Turning away from him, I quietly latched the door, slipping the deadbolt in place.

"What are you doing?"

I turned to face him and removed the gun from the back of my jeans.

He stumbled back, eyes widening. "Emilia, I'm your father. You can't—"

"Matteo killed her." I flipped off the safety. "But you, her father, let him." I lifted the gun, and he started rambling, trying to reason with me, but I was beyond reason. I wanted blood. I wanted justice. "And that makes you just as guilty, if not more."

I pulled the trigger, the bang exploding around the room. So easy, a single moment to end a life. For a second, it was like the world paused. And then, like a burst bubble, time resumed, my own thrumming pulse, my father's staggered breath. A small red patch started on his shirt and spread, creeping down the pale-blue material like lightning trying to find earth. He fell to the floor, clutching at his chest as though he could put all that blood back into his body.

I didn't know why I did it, but I lowered to the floor beside him and took his hand, not for this man, but for the man who had once read me stories and played hide and seek with us in the woods. He blinked up at me as breaths rattled his lungs. I knew I should feel something, but I didn't. I was just... devoid. I was vaguely aware of his men trying to hammer down the door, but it didn't matter. Blood pooled across the hardwood floor, soaking into the material of my jeans. I didn't care.

"I'm sorry," he whispered. "I'm sorry, Emi."

I said nothing, simply clutched his blood-slicked fingers in mine and held his hand as the man who raised me died. And a vicious little voice in the back of my head said it was more than Chiara had. More than he deserved. When his breaths rattled, and his chest finally fell for the last time, *that* was when I broke. The ugly, wrenching sobs of a girl who had lost her sister and killed her father for it. It was the anguish of someone who had seen and done things no one should have to.

I heard gunshots outside the room, but I didn't care if they killed me. My only regret would be that I didn't get to end Sergio and Matteo, but I knew Gio would. As absolutely as I knew the sun would rise in the morning.

23

GIO

The elevator doors opened on Donato's floor, and I stepped out into a scene of pure carnage. Two men were dead outside Sergio's suite, the door wide open and another body sprawled over the threshold. A few of my guys were already securing the floor. Adamo stood front and center, the young soldier cowering a little when he saw me.

"What the fuck is going on?"

"They were going to kill her. Philippe said you wanted her unharmed."

Fucking Emilia. Of course, she'd be knee-deep and in the middle of this. I wanted to wrap my hands around her pretty little neck until she turned purple. That was, until I truly absorbed his words, and a newfound rage pulsed through me at the thought. Traitor or not, she was still mine, and they had dared to try to hurt her…

"What do you mean they were going to kill her?"

"You'll see." He jerked his head toward the suite and walked back down the hall.

I stepped over the bodies and blood soaking into the carpet, trying not to get it on my boots. When I rounded the corner, I found Roberto Donato. His thousand-yard stare fixed on the ceiling as he lay in a pool of his own blood. And huddled in the corner was Emilia, knees pulled to her chest, cheek resting on them as she silently watched her father's body, as though he may magically come back to life. Though judging by my gun clutched in her white-knuckled grip, she was ready to put him right back down again. All evidence pointed to the fact that she had killed her father. Either she never had any idea about her uncle's plans, or she knew and changed her allegiance. But if she *didn't* know her uncle was a traitorous bastard, then she had just risked starting a whole new war by killing an Outfit underboss in my city.

I should have been mad, but any anger I felt evaporated the moment I took in her puffy eyes, silent tears cutting tracks down her blood-smudged cheeks. I had to wonder what had pushed her to this because, for all her fight, Emilia was not a killer.

"Piccola." I dropped to a crouch in front of her and pried the gun from her stiff fingers. When I touched her cheek, she blinked, her broken gaze meeting mine. She looked haunted. If she'd just spoken to me, I could have stopped this. If I'd thought she really wanted this, I would have pulled the trigger myself.

I turned toward the door where Adamo lingered. "Get a clean-up in here and get rid of these bodies." I glanced at Roberto. "Call Jackson to come get Roberto." I would decide what to do with him later. One thing was for sure, Sergio would never know it was Emilia who'd killed his brother.

When he turned away, I scooped up Emilia. She seemed so small and fragile in my arms. My little kitten clung to me like I was a safe harbor in a stormy sea, and I always would be for her. I walked her into a bathroom, and the second I placed her down onto the tiled shower floor, her legs buckled. She slid down the wall, eyes wide. I was pretty sure she was going into shock. Of course, she was going into shock; she'd just killed her own father.

"Emilia?"

She said nothing as I pulled her shirt over her head and began washing the blood off her. Pink-tinged water cascaded over her bare breasts before soaking into her blood-caked jeans and coming away crimson.

"Emilia, look at me." I pressed my finger beneath her chin. "Are you hurt?"

She didn't answer, but I couldn't see any injuries.

"You gonna tell me what happened?"

The sound of the water splashing over her body was my only answer. Questions burned through my mind, and if she were anyone else... But she wasn't anyone else. She was mine. And still every bit as innocent and scared as when I'd first found her in that motel room with a gun to her head. Too innocent for blood and murder and wars she didn't understand.

"I killed him," she whispered.

On a sigh, I dropped onto my ass beside her, the water soaking through my jeans. I pulled her into my lap and clutched her to my chest. "It's okay, piccola."

And that was when she fell apart.

Ugly sobs wracked her whole body, fingers knotting in my shirt like she couldn't get close enough, like I could save her from her torment. And I would try. I would hold her and piece her back together and never let her go because I was falling in love with her. And love drove men to madness.

To Be Continued...

I hope you love Gio and Emilia. I simply couldn't rush their story in one book, so you can pre-order A VOW OF LOVE AND VENGEANCE here, or wait for it to be released in the spring. (Sorry! I promise to make it worth the wait.) A war is coming, and so are some major spankings. 😈

W hile you wait, why not read Una and Nero's story? Russian assassin meets Italian capo and a whole lot of violent lust. Read KISS OF DEATH here. Free in KU.

ACKNOWLEDGMENTS

Huge thank you to you, my reader, for buying/ borrowing and reading the book.

I have to give a special mention to my beta/ PA/ friend, Kerry Fletcher for this one. This past year has been a nightmare for me. I have struggled to write, to plot, to get my juju back. She helped me get this book to where it is. From reading chapters to late night phone calls with me talking at her. I love you, Kerry, and you are the best.

And of course, my bestie, Stevie J. Cole is always there with wine chats.

Thank you to editor, Stephie Walls, proof reader, Autumn Jones, photographer Wander Aguilar, and model, Sol.

And of course, thank you to all the bloggers, Bookstagrammers, Booktoker's etc who show so much passion for authors books, and shout about them. You guys are the unsung hero's of the book world.

ALSO BY LP LOVELL

Sign up to my newsletter and stay up to date with new releases:

Join the Mailing List

Dark Mafia Series:

Kiss of Death series

Collateral Series

Touch of Death Series

Wrong Series

Bad Series

Standalones

Super Dark and Fucked Up:

Absolution

The Pope

The Game

Gritty High School Romance:

No Prince

No Good

Taboo Erotic Romance:

Dirty Boss

Website: www.lplovell.co.uk

Facebook: https://www.facebook.com/lplovellauthor

Instagram: @lp_lovell

TikTok: @authorlplovell

Goodreads: https://www.goodreads.com/author/show/7850247.LP_Lovell

Amazon: https://www.amazon.com/LP-Lovell/e/B00NDZ61PM

Printed in Great Britain
by Amazon